CRESSIDA BLYTHEWOOD

The Marquess's Unexpected Bride

Copyright © 2024 by Cressida Blythewood

All rights reserved. No part of this publication may be reproduced, stored or transmitted in any form or by any means, electronic, mechanical, photocopying, recording, scanning, or otherwise without written permission from the publisher. It is illegal to copy this book, post it to a website, or distribute it by any other means without permission.

This novel is entirely a work of fiction. The names, characters and incidents portrayed in it are the work of the author's imagination. Any resemblance to actual persons, living or dead, events or localities is entirely coincidental.

First edition

This book was professionally typeset on Reedsy.
Find out more at reedsy.com

Contents

1	The Morning Scandal	1
2	A Most Inconvenient Awakening	3
3	Tea and Tactical Maneuvers	7
4	The Perfect Storm	11
5	A Flash of Schemes and Desperation	15
6	The Fury	19
7	The Guilt and Guile	23
8	A Tangle of Scandal and Steel	27
9	Shadows of Friendship and Regret	31
10	The Bitter Taste of Regret	35
11	Caught Between Scandal and Sacrifice	39
12	The Faint Praise and False Promises	43
13	The Calm Before the Storm	47
14	A Perfectly Orchestrated Disaster	50
15	The Unraveling	55
16	Shattered Trust	59
17	A Hollow Promise	63
18	The Price of Deceit	66
19	The Burdens and Boundaries	69
20	The Unsettling Union	72
21	A Heavy Band	76
22	A Game of Patience	79
23	The Night of Seduction	84
24	The Morning Light	90
25	The Unexpected Ache	94
26	The Weight of Regret	97

27	The Weight of a Lie	101
28	The Shattered Illusion	105
29	A Crumbling Trust	111
30	A Desperate Heart	114
31	The Grip of Fear	118
32	A Fragile Hope	121
33	The Internal Struggle	125
34	The Breaking Point	129
35	The Reckoning	135
36	A Night of Shadows and Screams	138
37	The Absence	143
38	The Confrontation	147
39	The Desperate Search	150
40	A Glimmer of Hope	154
41	The Unexpected Reunion	158
42	A Simple Sanctuary	165
43	Healing and Forgiveness	169
44	The Homecoming	174
45	Double the Miracle, Double the Fear	178
46	A New Beginning	182
	About the Author	185
	Also by Cressida Blythewood	186

1

The Morning Scandal

I opened my eyes as a soft tickling sensation brushed against my face, followed by the warmth of breath fanning my skin. The moment I stirred, I realized something—or rather someone—was holding me tightly. Not just anyone, but a man. My heart skipped a beat as I recognized the strong, familiar arms of Colin Ashford, the Marquess of Ashford, who was still deep in sleep beside me, his embrace firm and intimate.

Memories from the previous night flooded back with startling clarity. The ball at Marquess Hawthorne's Manor had been a grand affair, filled with laughter, dancing, and far too much champagne. Colin and I had stayed together as the night grew late, drinking heavily and sharing more than a few secrets. But how had we ended up here, in a guest chamber, unclothed and entwined?

The room around us, opulent and richly decorated with heavy velvet drapes and dark mahogany furniture, was unfamiliar—a guest room in Hawthorne Manor, where servants were sure to begin their duties early in the morning. Panic tightened in my chest as I realized the risk we were in. If anyone found us like this, the scandal would be unavoidable, and the consequences unthinkable.

"Colin?!" I hissed urgently, trying to shake him awake.

He stirred slightly, mumbling something about his butler, but I couldn't wait for him to wake naturally. I patted him harder, nearly frantic, until his eyes finally fluttered open. He blinked at me in confusion before his gaze dropped, and he saw the reality of our situation. His eyes widened in shock.

"Anne..." he whispered, his voice trembling as he took in our state of undress. Realization dawned on him, and he nearly squealed in panic.

Without thinking, I clamped my hand over his mouth, silencing him before he could alert the entire household. "Colin, we need to get dressed. Now," I whispered fiercely, my heart pounding in my ears.

We both scrambled out from under the covers, desperately searching for our clothes, which were scattered haphazardly around the room like remnants of our lost self-control. My gown was crumpled on the floor, and my undergarments were draped over a chair as if tossed there carelessly. Colin found his shirt tangled around the bedpost, his trousers halfway across the room.

Just as we began to collect our garments, the door suddenly swung open. We froze in place, horror-stricken, as three servants stepped into the room. Their eyes widened in shock, and they screamed in unison at the sight of us—naked, disheveled, and undeniably compromised.

One of the maids, her face pale and trembling, turned and fled the room, her screams echoing down the corridor as she ran to spread the scandalous news of what she had just witnessed.

As the door slammed shut behind them, leaving Colin and me in stunned silence, I realized the full weight of what had just happened. The scandal would spread like wildfire, and by nightfall, the entire ton would know that Anne Blair and Colin Ashford had been found in a most compromising position.

There was no going back now. The course of my life had just irrevocably changed, and I could only imagine the storm that was about to descend upon us both.

2

A Most Inconvenient Awakening

I never imagined waking up in the morning at my best friend's manor after a grand party, and certainly not like this. The most astonishing thing—aside from the dull throb in my temples—was that I woke up naked, and not alone. No, I was sharing the bed with Anne Blair—not just any woman, but my best friend's older sister and Duke Bastian's sister-in-law. Yes, Anne Blair, the epitome of grace and composure, who I had always regarded with a mixture of respect and awe. And yet, here we were, lying together in a state of undress that could only spell disaster.

But here we were, tangled in bed sheets and utterly exposed, when the door burst open and the shrill screams of the servants filled the room. I was too stunned to react. I mean, how could I? The whole situation was so surreal that my brain was struggling to process it. The last thing I remembered was having a few too many drinks at Marquess Hawthorne's ball. Everything after that was a blur.

The previous night was a fog in my mind—a blur of dancing, laughter, and far too much champagne at Marquess Hawthorne's Manor. But the details were elusive, and no amount of squinting at the opulent surroundings was going to bring them back to me.

Before I could fully grasp the enormity of the situation, the door to the room burst open, and the piercing shriek of a maid cut through the air like a knife. My heart dropped into my stomach as I realized we had been discovered.

Anne, whose eyes widened in horror, quickly pulled the sheets up to cover herself.

As the screams echoed through the manor, Marchioness Hawthorne swept into the room, her expression a mix of shock and determined composure. She was a woman of swift action, and without uttering a single word, she strode to the bed, throwing a robe over Anne's shoulders and pulling her to her feet.

"Anne, come with me," the Marchioness commanded, her voice low and steady, as if she were dealing with nothing more than a misplaced teacup. But the urgency in her eyes betrayed her true feelings.

Anne, still disoriented, allowed herself to be led out of the room, clutching the robe tightly around her. The door closed behind them with a decisive click, leaving me alone with my spiraling thoughts and the deepening dread of what this scandal could mean for us both.

Before I could dwell on it any further, Marquess Matthew Hawthorne stormed into the room, his face a mask of barely contained fury. Without a word, he grabbed my clothes from where they were strewn across the floor and threw them at me with such force that I nearly stumbled back.

"Get dressed, Colin. For God's sake, stop lounging about naked in my house," Matthew snapped, his voice laced with irritation as he folded his arms across his chest.. "And stop standing there like a fool."

I hurriedly pulled on my trousers, my mind racing as I tried to think of something to say. But what explanation could I possibly offer? The last thing I remembered was the ball, the endless flow of champagne, and Anne—her laughter, her presence, and then... nothing.

"I don't care how this happened," he said, his tone stern but not unkind. "But I need to know—why on earth were you sleeping with Miss Blair? And before you say anything stupid, remember that she's your best friend older sister."

I opened my mouth to respond but quickly closed it, realizing I had absolutely no explanation. "Matthew, I... I honestly don't know," I finally admitted, shaking my head in bewilderment. "I have no memory of how this happened."

Matthew, his arms crossed tightly over his chest, watched me with a penetrating gaze. The tension in the room was palpable, thick enough to cut with a knife. Finally, he spoke, his voice low and simmering with frustration.

"Then, do you have any idea what you've done?" he demanded, each word laced with accusation. "Anne is Duke Bastian's sister-in-law. You've not just compromised her; you've entangled yourself with one of the most powerful men in the realm."

At the mention of Duke Bastian's name, a cold knot formed in my stomach. The Duke was a man of immense influence and authority, someone I had never had cause to think much about until he married my best friend, Adelaide. Since that union, however, something in me had shifted—a bitterness, a resentment that I could never quite put into words. And now, the thought of facing him over this... it was enough to make my insides churn.

Matthew's voice cut through my spiraling thoughts, bringing me back to the harsh reality of the moment. "Colin, if Bastian hears about this—"

"I know," I interrupted, not wanting to hear the rest. The very idea made my head throb harder. "But Matthew, I swear I don't remember how any of this happened."

Matthew's expression softened slightly, though his frustration remained evident. He let out a long, weary sigh, his shoulders sagging just a fraction. "This is a disaster, Colin. You've put both yourself and Anne in an impossible position. We need to figure out how to handle this before it spirals out of control."

I finished buttoning my shirt, my hands trembling slightly as I fumbled with the buttons. "Matthew, I... I truly have no memory of how we ended up here. The last thing I remember is the party, the drinks... and then nothing."

"Well, whatever the reason, this is a mess. You'd better hope we can contain it before the whole of London gets wind of it. For both your sakes!"

"I know, Matthew. I can't think right now, so just do what you think is right!"

Matthew studied me for a long moment, his gaze sharp and assessing. Finally, he nodded, though the worry in his eyes remained. "Then we need to control the narrative before it gets out. The servants will talk—hell, they've probably already started—but we can still manage this if we act quickly."

He paused, his expression hardening again. "But Colin, you need to understand what's at stake here. This isn't just about you and Anne. If this gets out, it could drag Duke Bastian into the scandal as well, and that is something none of us can afford."

The weight of his words settled heavily on my shoulders, and I nodded, understanding the gravity of the situation. "You're right. We need to contain this."

Matthew's expression softened slightly, though his resolve was clear. "I'll speak with Anne and see what she remembers. In the meantime, you need to stay out of sight—at least until we've figured out our next steps."

I nodded again, feeling a cold sweat break out across my skin. As I finished dressing, the full enormity of what had just happened began to sink in. What started as a night of revelry had turned into a nightmare—one that could ruin both my reputation and Anne's, and possibly drag Duke Bastian into a scandal none of us could afford.

As Matthew turned to leave the room, he glanced back at me, his expression a mix of concern and determination. "We'll find a way out of this, Colin. But it's going to take careful planning and swift action. And whatever happens, you need to be prepared to face the consequences."

I watched him go, the door closing behind him with a heavy thud. Alone once more, I sat on the edge of the bed, my mind reeling. This was no ordinary scandal. It was the kind that could change lives—ruin them, even. And the worst part was, I had no idea how to fix it.

3

Tea and Tactical Maneuvers

The morning air was still thick with the remnants of last night's revelry as I followed Marchioness Eleanor Hawthorne out of the room. The sound of the maid's scream still echoed in my ears, a sharp reminder of the disaster that had befallen me. My heart pounded furiously in my chest, each beat a frantic rhythm as I clutched the robe tighter around my trembling body.

Eleanor moved with a quiet urgency, her back straight, her movements efficient as she led me down the winding corridors of Hawthorne Manor. Her composure was as reassuring as it was daunting; she had always been known for her calm, unflappable demeanor. This morning, that reputation was on full display as she orchestrated what felt like a carefully planned escape.

We reached a smaller, private room—one I had not been in before—and Eleanor opened the door with the grace of a seasoned hostess. She gestured for me to enter, and as soon as we were inside, she closed the door firmly behind us, locking out the world and, for a brief moment, the scandal that threatened to engulf me.

"Sit, Anne," Eleanor instructed gently, guiding me to a plush armchair by the fireplace. Her voice was calm, steady—exactly what I needed in that moment. "I'll have the maid bring warm water and fresh clothes."

I nodded mutely, too overwhelmed to argue. The room was modest compared to the grandiose splendor of the rest of the manor, but its simplicity was comforting. The walls were lined with well-worn books, and the scent of lavender lingered in the air, soothing the frayed edges of my nerves.

Within minutes, a maid appeared, her expression carefully neutral as she carried a basin of warm water and a selection of clothes. Eleanor dismissed her with a subtle nod after instructing her to return with tea once I was dressed. The girl departed swiftly, leaving me alone with Eleanor.

She busied herself with the basin, dipping a cloth into the water and wringing it out before handing it to me. "Here, clean yourself up," she said softly, her tone devoid of judgment. "You'll feel better once you're dressed."

I accepted the cloth with shaking hands, grateful for the warmth it provided. As I dabbed at my face and neck, the coolness of the water slowly bringing me back to reality, Eleanor busied herself with selecting a gown for me from the clothes the maid had brought. She chose a simple dress, elegant but understated—exactly what was needed for the situation.

When I had finished washing up, Eleanor helped me into the dress, her hands swift and practiced. She worked in silence, which allowed the weight of what had happened to settle more heavily on my shoulders. I couldn't shake the gnawing fear of the scandal that could arise from this morning's events, nor could I ignore the shame that twisted in my stomach like a knife.

Once I was dressed, Eleanor stepped back and studied me with a critical eye. Satisfied, she gave a small nod. "There, much better," she said with a soft smile, though the concern in her eyes was unmistakable. "Now, come. Let's have some tea."

She led me to a cozy sitting room just down the hall, where a low table had been set with a fine porcelain tea service. The room was bathed in the gentle morning light, a stark contrast to the darkness I felt inside. I sat down gingerly, the soft cushions beneath me doing little to ease the tension in my spine.

Eleanor poured the tea with the grace of someone who had hosted countless such gatherings, though this one was far from the usual social calls. She handed me a cup, her movements steady and deliberate, and I accepted it with both hands, grateful for something to hold onto.

"I must apologize, Eleanor," I began, my voice barely above a whisper. "I never meant to... soil your house with my... my naughty actions with Colin." The words tasted bitter on my tongue, but I forced them out, my shame deepening with each syllable.

Eleanor, however, simply smiled—gently, almost motherly. "There's no need for apologies, Anne," she replied, her tone warm and understanding. "These things happen. Everyone makes mistakes."

Her kindness was almost unbearable. I had expected scorn, anger even, but Eleanor had none of it. Instead, she seemed intent on reassuring me, and I clung to her words like a lifeline.

"But what about the scandal?" I asked, my voice trembling. "The servants... they saw us. How can we keep this quiet?"

Eleanor took a delicate sip of her tea, her eyes never leaving mine. "The servants will be dealt with," she said calmly. "I'll make sure that they understand the importance of discretion. They know better than to gossip about the guests of this house—especially when it concerns something as sensitive as this."

Her confidence was soothing, but I couldn't help but worry. "And what about everyone else? Surely people will ask why I stayed the night..."

"I'll take care of that as well," Eleanor assured me. "We'll say that you overslept and decided to stay here for the night. It's a perfectly reasonable explanation, especially after a party like last night's. No one will think twice about it."

"But the truth... the truth about what happened between Colin and me..."

"Must be kept a secret," Eleanor finished for me, her tone firm but kind. "For your sake, and for Colin's. No one else needs to know the details of what happened this morning. It's in everyone's best interest that this remains between us."

I nodded slowly, knowing she was right. Whatever had transpired between Colin and me, it was something that could destroy us both if it became public knowledge. Keeping it hidden was the only option.

"Thank you, Eleanor," I said quietly, my gratitude genuine. "I don't know what I would have done without your help."

She reached across the table and placed her hand over mine, giving it a reassuring squeeze. "Think nothing of it, my dear," she said softly. "We all find ourselves in difficult situations from time to time. The important thing is how we handle them. And you," she added with a small, approving smile, "are handling this with far more grace than most."

I returned her smile and sipped the tea. "Yes, you're right, Eleanor."

4

The Perfect Storm

The instant I stepped out of Hawthorne Manor, wrapped in borrowed finery and shrouded in a carefully constructed lie, I knew the path I had chosen was not one for the faint of heart. The scandal I had sown that morning, carefully veiled under the guise of an innocent mistake, was my escape route—a calculated maneuver in the grand chess game of London society. The soft, maternal concern in Marchioness Eleanor Hawthorne's eyes might have soothed someone else, but I had no need for comfort. I needed only one thing: for the world to know.

As Eleanor had promised, she took swift action. The gossiping maid was dismissed before noon, and word was sent out that I had simply overslept after the previous night's festivities. The story was believable enough—a young woman of good standing taking refuge in a friend's home after a long evening. But as the hours passed and the house remained unnervingly silent, I realized that the marchioness's well-meaning attempts at discretion were smothering my carefully laid plans.

This wouldn't do at all.

With the maid's hasty departure and the servants all suitably cowed, there was no whisper of scandal yet stirring in the air. And how could there be? Eleanor's iron grip on her household ensured that all was quiet, that appearances were maintained, that my reputation remained intact. But what Eleanor saw as protection, I saw as interference. This scandal was meant to save me from a fate worse than social ruin—an unwanted marriage to a man like Earl Eric Blackwood. It was supposed to be my weapon, not my downfall.

So, I took matters into my own hands.

While Eleanor tended to her guests and made arrangements to send me home discreetly, I slipped away from the watchful eyes of the remaining servants and made my way back to the scene of the crime—Colin's room, where the remnants of our supposed tryst still lay scattered like breadcrumbs. It was too easy, really. A few misplaced whispers, a quick word to the footman, a casual mention of the morning's events to the chatty scullery maid. The rumors began to spin themselves, building momentum as they traveled from one loose tongue to another.

By the time I left Hawthorne Manor, the spark had been ignited. The servants, for all their fear of Eleanor's wrath, couldn't resist the allure of a good scandal—especially one involving the Marquess of Ashford and a woman of my standing. I could practically feel the gossip spreading like wildfire, the words twisting and turning with each retelling until they became something altogether more salacious.

And that was exactly what I wanted.

Back at Windermere Manor, I settled into the role of the sweet, innocent daughter—dutifully demure, as expected by my parents and society at large. I took tea with my mother, attended to my daily tasks, and smiled politely at the endless parade of callers who came to pay their respects. But behind my carefully crafted mask, I waited. Waited for the whispers to reach the ears of the ton, for the rumors to swell into a tidal wave that no amount of discretion could contain.

It didn't take long.

Within days, the scandal exploded across London like a carefully placed charge. The ton buzzed with the news, the tale growing more lurid and sensational with each passing hour. It was no longer just a rumor; it was a full-blown scandal, and my name was on every pair of lips that mattered.

It was at one of my mother's afternoon teas that I heard the first confirmation that my plan was working. The drawing room was filled with the gentle hum of conversation, the clinking of china, and the soft rustle of skirts as the ladies of society exchanged pleasantries. But the atmosphere was thick with anticipation, an undercurrent of excitement that suggested something far more interesting than tea and biscuits was on the agenda.

I didn't have to wait long.

One of the ladies—an acquaintance of my mother's known for her love of gossip—leaned in, her eyes alight with barely contained glee. "Have you heard the latest, Lady Windermere?" she asked, her voice a conspiratorial whisper that carried just far enough to reach my ears. "They say the Marquess of Ashford was found in quite the compromising position with a young lady— someone most unexpected."

I held my breath, but only for effect. My mother's eyes flicked to me, and I could see the tension in her posture, the way her fingers tightened around her teacup. "Oh?" she replied, her tone carefully neutral. "And who might this young lady be?"

The woman's smile widened. "Why, Miss Anne Blair, of course. Though I'm sure it's just a misunderstanding... or perhaps, a lapse in judgment?"

I let the tiniest of gasps escape my lips, just loud enough for the others to hear. It was a delicate sound, perfectly timed to draw attention without seeming deliberate. "Surely not," I murmured, my voice tinged with the perfect blend of shock and hurt. "There must be some mistake."

But I knew there was no mistake. Not anymore. The game had begun, and the pieces were falling into place exactly as I had planned.

My mother, bless her, tried to defend my honor. "My daughter is a lady of impeccable conduct," she said sharply, her eyes narrowing at the other woman. "She would never be involved in such an indecent affair."

"Of course, of course," the woman agreed, though her tone was anything but convinced. "But you know how people talk. And with the Marquess being such a... sought-after bachelor, well, these things tend to get out of hand."

I pretended to be mortified, lowering my gaze as if I couldn't bear the weight of the accusation. But inside, I was triumphant. The scandal was spreading just as I had intended. Soon, it would reach every corner of London, leaving Colin no choice but to act.

The truth was, this scandal was my escape plan, my carefully orchestrated path to freedom. I had no intention of ending up like the other women in my position—shunted into an arranged marriage with a man who viewed me as nothing more than a prize to be won. I wanted control over my future, and if that meant playing the part of the scandalous schemer, then so be it.

As I took a delicate bite of a biscuit, I allowed myself a small, secret smile. The wheels were in motion, and there was no turning back now. The gossip, the scandal, the whispers—they were all part of the plan. Soon, Colin would come to me, driven by the very rumors I had set into motion. And when he did, I would be ready.

Let the ton talk. Let them whisper and speculate. For in the end, it was I who would have the last word.

5

A Flash of Schemes and Desperation

The chattering voices of the ladies at tea faded into the background as my mind wandered back to the circumstances that had driven me to orchestrate the scandal now spreading through London like wildfire. As I nibbled on a biscuit, the familiar faces and polite conversation around me dissolved, replaced by the memory of a different, darker conversation that had taken place only weeks earlier.

It was the night Adelaide made her announcement. My younger sister, the golden child of the Blair family, had shared the news that she was expecting her first child. She glowed with happiness, radiating the kind of contentment that only a woman in love, secure in her marriage, could. Adelaide was the beloved wife of Duke Bastian Lightwood, a man of immense power and influence, feared and respected in equal measure. As soon as she shared the news, our parents were overcome with joy, showering her with praises and blessings. The air was thick with congratulations and well-wishes, and for a moment, it felt as though the entire room had been lit by her happiness.

But as Adelaide's star rose ever higher, the pressure on me grew unbearable. At twenty-five, I was no longer the belle of the ball, no longer the fresh debutante with a full dance card. I was, in the eyes of society, a woman on the brink of becoming an old maid. Adelaide's marriage and impending motherhood had only sharpened the focus on my own unmarried state. If the younger Miss Blair could secure such a match, what was wrong with the elder?

As the evening wound down and the family gathered in the parlor, the smiles my parents had worn so easily began to fade as they turned their attention to me. The warmth that had filled the room moments before seemed to dissipate, replaced by a cold, pointed silence as my parents exchanged glances that spoke volumes.

"Anne," my father began, his voice heavy with duty and disappointment. "You know how much we care for you, but you must realize that time is not on your side."

My mother, seated beside him, nodded solemnly. "We only want what's best for you, dear. But the longer you wait, the fewer your options become. Now that Adelaide is happily settled, it's time we think seriously about your future."

The implication was clear: if I didn't act soon, my chances of a respectable marriage would dwindle to nothing. The whispers in society were already growing louder, questioning why I, Anne Blair, still remained unwed while my younger sister thrived in wedded bliss.

My parents, as always, had no shortage of suggestions, each more dreadful than the last. Mr. Timothy Crawford was at the top of their list—a widower from Whitby, with five unruly sons to raise on his own. His wife had passed away not long ago, and while he had originally proposed to Adelaide, my parents now saw him as a suitable match for me. After all, I was "of an age" where such considerations—like raising another woman's children—should be secondary to securing a husband.

The thought of spending my days managing his countryside estate and disciplining his rambunctious brood made my stomach churn. Mr. Crawford, with his perpetual air of fatigue and a baby practically still in swaddling clothes, was far from the life I had envisioned for myself. It wasn't just the drudgery of the task that repelled me—it was the idea of giving up everything I was, everything I wanted, to fulfill society's narrow expectations.

But there was another option, one that was equally distasteful, though for different reasons. Earl Eric Blackwood, a man of high rank but low morals, had made his interest in me known in the most appalling way. His reputation as a rake was well-earned, with whispers of gambling debts, illicit affairs, and even an illegitimate child circulating in every corner of the ton. His connection to Duke Bastian Lightwood, my sister's powerful husband, only complicated matters further. Rejecting his proposal outright could create a rift between the families, something my parents were desperate to avoid.

I knew what was expected of me. I was supposed to smile, nod demurely, and accept the role of wife—whether to Mr. Crawford, the weary widower, or to Earl Eric, the scandal-ridden rake. I was supposed to sacrifice my dreams, my independence, and my desires on the altar of duty and social propriety.

But why should I?

Why should I settle for a life that held no joy, no passion, no meaning beyond fulfilling the expectations of others? Why should I bind myself to a man who saw me as nothing more than a means to an end, whether that end was an orderly household or a trophy wife? I was Anne Blair, not some simpering, witless girl to be married off to the highest bidder.

As the pressure mounted, a simmering anger began to grow within me—a quiet, burning rage at the unfairness of it all. And with that anger came clarity. I would not let myself be shackled to a life I didn't choose. I would take control of my own destiny, even if it meant playing a role I had never imagined for myself.

It was in that moment of desperation and defiance that the idea had taken root. Colin Ashford, the Marquess of Ashford and Adelaide's best friend, was the answer. Colin, with his easy charm, his honorable reputation, and his deep connection to our family, was the perfect candidate for my plan. If I could engineer a scandal between us—one that would leave him no choice but to marry me—I could escape the clutches of Mr. Crawford and Earl Eric. I could secure my future on my terms.

Colin was more than just a marquess; he was Adelaide's closest friend, the one she had confided in for years. His connection to my sister made him an ideal target for my scheme. If I could orchestrate a situation where Colin and I were discovered in a compromising position, there would be no question of our marriage—especially with Adelaide's inevitable influence over her husband, Duke Bastian. It was a simple equation: Colin's honor would leave him no choice but to marry me, and my family would have to accept it.

That night had been a masterstroke of deception. I had known that Colin wouldn't willingly cooperate with my plan, so I had taken matters into my own hands. A few drops of a potent drug in his drink, something subtle enough not to arouse suspicion but strong enough to make him lose control quickly, and Colin had been putty in my hands. He had barely been conscious when I led him to the room, his resistance weak and muddled by the effects of the drug. Once inside, it had been easy enough to undress him and position us both in the bed, creating the perfect scene for the inevitable discovery.

The morning at Hawthorne Manor had been the culmination of that plan. But when Marchioness Eleanor Hawthorne's intervention threatened to quash the scandal before it had time to take hold, I knew I had to act quickly. The rumors I had spread were no accident—they were a carefully calculated move in a game I was determined to win.

Now, as I sat in the drawing room, the echoes of my parents' disappointment still ringing in my ears, I smiled to myself. The scandal was doing its work, and soon Colin would have no choice but to act. The wheels were in motion, and I was in control.

This was my escape, my salvation. And I would see it through to the very end, no matter the cost.

6

The Fury

The tea had barely cooled in its delicate porcelain cup when I sensed the shift in my mother's demeanor. Lady Windermere, always so composed, always so careful to maintain the appearance of calm authority, now eyed me with an intensity that sent a prickle of unease down my spine. She had heard the whispers—the same whispers I had carefully planted—and now, it seemed, she intended to confront me about them.

As the last of our guests took their leave, exchanging pleasantries that felt as hollow as they were insincere, I braced myself for what I knew was coming. The door closed behind them, and the silence that settled in the drawing room was thick, charged with unspoken tension.

"Anne," my mother began, her voice cool but edged with something sharper, something almost... fearful. "What are these rumors I've been hearing? This talk of you and Colin... Is it true?"

I hesitated, allowing my eyes to drop to my lap, my fingers twisting the handkerchief I had been holding. I could feel her gaze drilling into me, demanding answers I was more than prepared to give—but on my terms.

"Mother," I murmured, injecting just the right amount of tremor into my voice, "I'm... I'm so ashamed. I don't know how it happened, but... yes, the rumors are true."

Her reaction was immediate and visceral. Lady Windermere, who rarely let her emotions surface, visibly flinched as if I had struck her. Her breath caught, and her hands clenched into tight fists in her lap. For a moment, she simply stared at me, her mouth opening and closing as though searching for the right words and finding none.

"Anne," she finally said, her voice trembling with a mix of shock and confusion, "how could you? How could this happen? First Adelaide, and now you? What have I done to deserve this?"

I bit back a bitter smile. Adelaide's marriage to Duke Bastian had been the crown jewel of my mother's ambitions, the culmination of all her hopes and dreams for her daughters. But to hear her speak now, it was clear that even that triumph was tainted in her eyes, marred by the whispers of scandal that had surrounded Adelaide's engagement. And now, with me, the elder daughter, entangled in a similar web, it was as though her world was crumbling.

"But Adelaide's marriage to Bastian is hardly a scandal," I protested, feigning hurt. "She's a duchess, Mother. She married one of the most powerful men in the country."

"Yes," my mother snapped, her composure beginning to fray at the edges, "but do you forget the whispers that surrounded their engagement? The questions, the insinuations... I thought it would end there. I thought, at least with you, we wouldn't have to endure such shame again."

The bitterness in her voice was palpable, and I could see the anger simmering just beneath the surface. It was anger born not of concern for me, but of fear—fear for the family's reputation, fear of what the ton would say, fear of what this scandal would mean for her standing among the other ladies of society.

"Mother," I began, adopting a pleading tone, "I didn't mean for this to happen. I never intended for things to go this far, but... Colin is different. He's kind, honorable, and..."

"He's Adelaide's friend!" she interrupted, her voice rising as she leaned forward, her eyes blazing with fury. "He's like family to us, Anne! He's younger than you, practically a boy, and you... you've embroiled him in this mess?"

I straightened, my own anger beginning to rise in response. "I didn't embroil him in anything, Mother. Colin is a grown man, fully capable of making his own decisions. And as for our age difference, it's hardly scandalous. Many marriages have a greater disparity."

My mother's eyes narrowed, her lips thinning into a tight line. "Do not try to justify this, Anne. You know as well as I do that Colin has always been close to this family. He's practically one of us! And now you've gone and ruined that with your... your reckless behavior."

"I'm not reckless," I snapped back, my patience fraying. "I've done nothing wrong."

"Nothing wrong?" she echoed, her voice incredulous. "Nothing wrong? Do you have any idea what people are saying? That you were found in his bed, Anne! Unclothed, in a state of—"

"Mother, please," I interrupted, cutting her off before she could say more. "Whatever the rumors, the truth is that Colin and I... we care for each other. This isn't some meaningless dalliance."

But before she could respond, the door to the drawing room creaked open, and both of us turned to see Adelaide standing in the doorway, her face pale, her hand resting protectively on the swell of her belly. She was six months pregnant now, and the sight of her in such a delicate state sent a pang of guilt through me, brief as it was.

"Is it true?" Adelaide asked, her voice soft but firm. "The scandal between you and Colin... is it true?"

For a moment, the room was silent, the air thick with the tension between the three of us. My mother's gaze darted between Adelaide and me, her anger momentarily giving way to uncertainty.

"Yes," I finally said, meeting Adelaide's eyes with a steadiness I didn't entirely feel. "It's true."

Adelaide's brow furrowed in confusion as she took a step closer. "But... Colin is my friend. He's... we've known him for so long. How could this happen?"

The hurt in her voice was unmistakable, and for a brief moment, I regretted the plan I had set in motion. But I couldn't afford to falter now, not when I was so close to achieving what I wanted.

"I'm sorry, Adelaide," I said softly, hoping my voice carried the right mix of contrition and resolve. "I never meant for this to hurt you. But sometimes... things happen that we can't control."

My mother's anger flared again, but before she could speak, Adelaide held up a hand, silencing her. "We'll figure this out," she said, her voice steady despite the turmoil in her eyes. "But we need to be careful, Anne. We can't let this ruin everything."

I nodded, though inside, I knew that the game was far from over. The pieces were moving, and soon enough, Colin would be forced to make a decision. And when he did, I would be ready.

7

The Guilt and Guile

The argument between my mother and me had left the room charged with a tense silence, the air thick with unresolved anger and the lingering sting of harsh words. Adelaide, standing there with her hand on her swollen belly, looked between us with wide, troubled eyes. The color had drained from her face, leaving her as pale as the delicate lace trim of her gown.

Before I could respond to her, she gasped softly, her hand moving to press more firmly against her abdomen. A flicker of fear shot through me as I saw the way her other hand gripped the back of a nearby chair for support.

"Adelaide?" my mother's voice was no longer filled with anger but with concern. She hurried to Adelaide's side, her previous fury seemingly forgotten. "What's wrong? Are you in pain?"

Adelaide nodded slightly, her breathing shallow and quick. "It's just... I'm not sure. It was a sharp pain, but it's easing now. Perhaps it's just the baby moving... or maybe I was just shocked by all of this."

The tension in the room shifted, the focus moving entirely to Adelaide's well-being. My mother immediately went into action, fussing over her, guiding her to sit down, and ordering a servant to bring a cool compress and some soothing tea. I stood to the side, watching as the scene unfolded, my own emotions in turmoil.

Guilt gnawed at me, a bitter taste in the back of my throat. I had never intended for Adelaide to be caught up in this. She was innocent in all of it, and seeing her in pain because of something I had orchestrated made me feel something uncomfortably close to regret. But regret, I reminded myself, was a luxury I could not afford.

Once Adelaide was settled, her breathing calm, and the color slowly returning to her cheeks, I knew I had to speak with her. This wasn't how I had imagined things would unfold. Adelaide was more than just my sister; she was my confidante, the one person I never wanted to deceive. I could fool the world, but Adelaide... I owed her the truth.

After my mother left the room to fetch the physician, I approached Adelaide, my heart heavy with the weight of what I was about to say—or rather, what I intended to say. But before I could even begin, Adelaide reached out and took my hand, pulling me into a gentle embrace. The warmth of her body, the steady rhythm of her breath, only deepened the ache of guilt in my chest.

"I'm so sorry, Anne," she whispered, her voice filled with genuine remorse. "I never meant for my scandal to cast a shadow over you. I didn't realize that what happened with Bastian would lead to this. If I had known, I would have been more careful... I would have done something to protect you."

Her words, spoken with such sincerity, pierced through me. She thought I was suffering because of her—because of the path she had taken with Duke Bastian. She believed that my current predicament was a direct result of the example she had set, and that if not for her, I would have been safe from such scandal.

Adelaide pulled back slightly, her hands resting on my shoulders as she looked into my eyes. "But it's going to be all right," she said, her voice stronger now, as if she were trying to convince herself as much as me. "I'll talk to Colin. I know him, Anne. He's a good man, and he cares about you. We'll figure this out together, and everything will be fine."

I opened my mouth to speak, to finally tell her the truth, to admit that I had engineered the entire situation, that Colin was innocent, and that this scandal was of my own making. But the words caught in my throat, strangled by the sight of Adelaide's earnest expression, the trust in her eyes.

How could I shatter that trust? How could I confess that I had used the very tactics she had been caught in, not out of love or desperation, but out of cold calculation? Adelaide had been a victim of circumstance, her love for Bastian born from genuine feeling, not from manipulation. And yet, here she was, ready to protect me, to take on the burden of my actions as if they were her own.

I couldn't do it. I couldn't tell her the truth.

Instead, I swallowed the confession, forcing it down along with the bitter taste of my guilt. I forced a smile, one that I hoped looked as sincere as the one Adelaide had given me. "Thank you, Adelaide," I whispered, my voice strained with the effort of holding back the truth. "I don't know what I'd do without you."

She smiled in return, a soft, loving smile that only deepened my sense of guilt. "You'll always have me, Anne. We're sisters. We take care of each other, no matter what."

She pulled me into another hug, and I let myself sink into the comfort of her embrace, even as the weight of my deception settled heavily on my shoulders. She had no idea that the situation was far worse than she imagined, that Colin had been dragged into this mess not by some unfortunate accident, but by my deliberate design.

As she held me, her hands gently patting my back, I closed my eyes and let out a slow breath. I had come so far, and there was no turning back now. Adelaide's words echoed in my mind, a mixture of comfort and condemnation.

Everything would be fine, she had said. We'll figure this out together, she had promised. But the truth was, I had already figured it out—long before the scandal had ever broken. I had known exactly what I was doing, and I had made my choice.

But as Adelaide released me, her eyes shining with determination, I couldn't help but wonder if I had miscalculated after all. For the first time since this all began, I felt the faint stirrings of doubt. Not in my plan, but in the cost it was exacting on those I cared about most.

I forced the doubt back, locked it away in the deepest part of my mind, and let Adelaide guide me to the settee. I couldn't afford to let emotions cloud my judgment now. I had to see this through to the end, no matter the cost.

And if that meant swallowing my guilt along with my confession, so be it.

8

A Tangle of Scandal and Steel

My head was pounding, a relentless, throbbing pain that no amount of rubbing at my temples could ease. I slumped back in the leather chair behind my desk, trying to make sense of the chaos that had suddenly taken over my life. The papers scattered before me—business ledgers, contracts, correspondence—felt like meaningless clutter. None of it mattered now, not with the scandal swirling around me, threatening to consume everything I'd worked so hard to build.

"Damn it," I muttered under my breath, pressing my hands harder into my temples. How had it all gone so wrong? How had I, Colin Ashford, the Marquess of Ashford, managed to land myself in the middle of such a sordid mess?

The answer eluded me, and the frustration gnawed at my insides like a hungry beast. I'd been hearing whispers, rumors that twisted and turned with every retelling, growing more outlandish and damaging by the hour. But I couldn't make sense of it. I couldn't recall a single moment that could have led to this... this disaster.

Harris, my butler, stood a few feet away, watching me with the quiet, measured gaze I'd come to rely on over the years. Harris had been with the Ashford family for decades, practically raised me after my parents passed, and if anyone could make sense of this madness, it was him. But even Harris seemed at a loss, his usually calm expression tinged with something that looked uncomfortably close to concern.

I finally looked up at him, feeling the anger simmering just below the surface. "Harris," I said, my voice rough with frustration, "what the hell is going on? I've been hearing about this blasted scandal for days, and I still don't understand how it happened. How did Anne and I end up... like this?"

Harris stepped forward, his tone respectful yet firm. "My lord, it appears that the incident at Marquess Hawthorne's manor has been... greatly exaggerated by the ton. The story that is circulating suggests that you and Miss Blair were discovered in a compromising position, leading to the assumption that you are... involved."

"Involved?" I echoed, incredulity dripping from the word. How could they think that? How could they twist something so innocent into something so... vile? "Harris, I have no memory of anything happening that night. I don't understand how this could have spiraled so out of control."

Harris nodded, his eyes full of sympathy I didn't want. "Indeed, my lord. However, the situation has escalated beyond mere gossip. The fact that Miss Blair is Duke Bastian's sister-in-law has only added fuel to the fire. People are talking, my lord, and the implications are... severe."

My headache pounded harder as Harris's words sank in. Anne—of all people. Adelaide's sister. How had I managed to drag her into this nightmare? "How is Anne?" I asked, a knot of worry tightening in my chest. "What is she doing? Has she said anything about all this?"

"Miss Blair has not left Windermere Manor since the scandal broke," Harris replied carefully. "From what I understand, she is being kept out of the public eye to avoid further damage to her reputation. The family is attempting to manage the situation, but the gossip has spread far and wide, and it is proving difficult to contain."

I clenched my jaw, the anger building inside me like a storm. I cared about Anne—how could I not? She was smart, sharp-witted, and had always carried herself with a grace that few could match. The thought that I might be responsible for ruining her reputation was unbearable. But as much as I hated what this was doing to Anne, there was more at stake. Much more.

Harris hesitated for a moment, then continued, his voice lowering to a grave tone. "There is more, my lord. As you know, the Ashford family's mining operations are closely tied to the jewelry business owned by Duke Bastian. The Duke's enterprises are some of the most successful in the realm, and his partnership with us has been crucial to maintaining the profitability of our mines. If Duke Bastian were to take offense at this scandal—if he were to perceive any slight or dishonor to his family—it could have dire consequences for our business."

The words hit me like a physical blow. The Ashford mines—our mines—were the cornerstone of our wealth, our legacy. Situated in the rugged hills of the North, the mines produced some of the finest gemstones in the country, gemstones that Duke Bastian's company, turned into coveted pieces of jewelry worn by nobility across Europe.

The partnership between our families had been mutually beneficial for years. The Duke's company provided a reliable and lucrative market for our gemstones, while the Ashford family ensured a steady supply of the finest gems. It was a relationship built on trust, respect—and now, I realized with a sickening jolt—fragility.

"If Duke Bastian were to withdraw his support," Harris said, his tone heavy with the gravity of the situation, "the impact on the Ashford family would be catastrophic. Without his business, the mines would struggle to find buyers for their gems, and the value of the operation would plummet. We could lose everything, my lord."

Everything. The word echoed in my mind, leaving me hollow. The thought of losing the mines—of losing everything generations of Ashfords had built—was terrifying. Our name was synonymous with wealth, with power. But without the mines, that legacy would crumble to dust.

"Are you telling me," I said slowly, my voice tight with barely controlled fury, "that this ridiculous scandal could ruin my family's entire fortune? All because of some baseless rumors?"

Harris nodded, his face grave. "I'm afraid so, my lord. Duke Bastian is a powerful man, and his influence extends far beyond the business world. If he believes that you have wronged his sister-in-law, he could choose to end the partnership. And without that partnership, the Ashford mines would suffer greatly."

My hands curled into fists, my knuckles turning white as I fought to keep my emotions in check. How had one night—one damned night that I couldn't even remember—turned my entire world upside down? How could everything fall apart so quickly, so irrevocably?

And Anne. I couldn't stop thinking about her, couldn't stop worrying about how she was handling all of this. The image of her, strong and composed, flashed in my mind, and I felt a pang of guilt. She didn't deserve this. None of us did.

A knock at the door interrupted my thoughts, and Harris stepped back as the door opened to reveal Adelaide. She stood there, her expression a mixture of concern and determination, her hand resting on the swell of her pregnant belly. Despite everything, she still carried herself with the grace and confidence that had always defined her.

"Adelaide," I said, my voice strained as I tried to push down the panic threatening to consume me. "What are you doing here?"

"I came to see you, Colin," she replied, stepping into the room with a calmness I envied. "We need to talk—about Anne, about this scandal. I'm worried, and I know you are too."

I leaned back in my chair, feeling the weight of the situation pressing down on me from all sides. Adelaide had always been a steadying force in my life, her presence like a balm for the chaos swirling around us. And now, with everything spiraling out of control, I needed that steadiness more than ever.

"Of course," I said quietly, rubbing my temples again as the relentless headache pounded in my skull. "Let's talk."

9

Shadows of Friendship and Regret

Adelaide closed the door behind her, shutting out the noise and chaos of the outside world, leaving just the two of us in the dimly lit study. The room felt smaller, more oppressive, with Adelaide standing there—six months pregnant, glowing with the life she carried, and yet, I could see the strain in her eyes. It was the kind of weariness that went beyond physical exhaustion, a weight that came from deep inside, from worries that words couldn't quite capture.

She crossed the room slowly, her hand still resting protectively over her belly, and I felt a pang in my chest—sharp, bitter, and so deeply buried I hadn't even realized it was there until this moment. Adelaide, my oldest friend, the woman I'd known since childhood, the one who had always been there, suddenly seemed so distant, so changed. The last time I'd seen her, it was at her wedding—a grand affair full of hope and promise. And now, she was here, standing before me, carrying another man's child.

I swallowed hard, forcing down the bile that rose in my throat. It should have been mine. The thought was treacherous, bitter, and entirely unbidden, but it was there all the same. It should have been my child she was carrying, not Duke Bastian's. I had never allowed myself to acknowledge it before, not even in the darkest corners of my mind. But now, standing here, watching her, the truth of it crashed over me like a wave.

"Colin," Adelaide said, her voice cutting through the haze of my thoughts.

There was a sharp edge to her tone, a hint of anger that she was struggling to contain. "I need to know the truth. I need you to tell me what happened between you and Anne."

I stared at her, at the way she held herself so rigidly, at the flicker of doubt in her eyes that tore at my heart. Adelaide, who had always trusted me implicitly, now looked at me as if I were a stranger, someone capable of causing harm to her beloved sister.

"Adelaide," I began, but the words felt thick and clumsy in my mouth. How could I explain something I didn't even understand myself? How could I make sense of the chaos when I was drowning in it?

She took a step closer, her eyes narrowing. "Don't lie to me, Colin. I know you. You've been my friend for years, since we were children. I never thought you would... that you could..." She trailed off, her voice shaking with the emotion she was trying to keep in check. "How could you do this to Anne? To me? I thought you were better than this."

The accusation hit me like a blow, knocking the breath from my lungs. How could I explain that I hadn't done anything—at least, not intentionally? How could I make her see that I was as lost and confused as she was?

"I didn't..." I started, but the words fell flat. What could I say? That I had no memory of what had happened? That I was just as shocked by the scandal as she was? It all sounded so hollow, so inadequate in the face of her pain.

Adelaide's gaze bore into me, searching for answers, for something—anything—that would make this all make sense. But I had nothing to give her, nothing that would ease the hurt I could see in her eyes.

She shook her head, her frustration boiling over. "Do you have any idea what this has done to Anne? To our family? The scandal is everywhere, Colin. People are talking, spreading lies, and now... now Anne's reputation is in tatters. And all because of you."

I felt a surge of helplessness, mixed with a bitter anger I had no right to feel. Yes, I had wanted Adelaide once—more than anything. But she had chosen someone else, and that was something I had accepted, or at least tried to. But to stand here now, accused of something so vile, something that went against everything I was, made my blood boil.

"Adelaide," I said, my voice low and controlled, "I didn't do what they're saying. I swear to you, I didn't touch Anne. I don't know how this happened, but I would never—"

"Then how do you explain it?" she demanded, cutting me off. "How do you explain being found in bed with her? How do you explain the gossip, the rumors, the damage to Anne's name? If you didn't do it, then who did? Who else would want to ruin her like this?"

I had no answer. No explanation. Only a seething frustration that made me want to punch something, to break through the fog of confusion and anger that clouded my mind. But I couldn't. I was trapped, cornered by a scandal I didn't understand and a woman I still cared for, who was looking at me like I was a monster.

"I don't know," I said finally, the words bitter on my tongue. "I don't know how it happened, but I didn't... I couldn't have done what they're saying. I would never hurt Anne. You have to believe me."

For a moment, there was silence. Adelaide's eyes softened, but the doubt was still there, lingering like a shadow. She wanted to believe me—I could see that. But the scandal had planted a seed of doubt, one that had taken root and refused to be dislodged.

She looked down at her hands, resting protectively over her unborn child, and I felt another pang of jealousy, one I had no right to feel. She was married, expecting a child, and living the life she had chosen. And I... I was still grappling with the what-ifs, the could-have-beens, and the bitter realization that the life I had once imagined was forever out of reach.

"Colin," she said softly, her voice tinged with sadness, "whether you meant to or not, you've hurt Anne. This scandal... it's tearing her apart. You owe it to her, to all of us, to make this right."

I nodded slowly, feeling the weight of responsibility settle on my shoulders. "I'll do whatever it takes," I said, the words heavy with resignation. "I'll clear Anne's name, Adelaide. I promise you that. But marriage... I don't think that's the answer."

Adelaide's eyes met mine, and for a moment, I thought she might argue, might insist that marriage was the only way to salvage what was left of Anne's reputation. But instead, she sighed, the tension draining from her posture as if she had expected nothing less.

"I understand," she said quietly. "But you have to do something, Colin. You have to take responsibility. If you don't, this scandal will destroy her. And if that happens... I don't know if I could ever forgive you."

The words were like a knife to the heart, but I nodded again, accepting the burden she had placed on me. I would clear Anne's name, no matter the cost, even if it meant sacrificing my own reputation in the process.

As I watched Adelaide leave the room, her figure now softened by the swell of pregnancy, I couldn't help but feel the cold hand of regret tighten its grip on my heart. I had wanted something else, something more, and now all I had was the responsibility of mending the broken pieces of a life that wasn't even mine to begin with.

But if this was the price I had to pay to make things right, then I would pay it. Even if it meant losing everything in the process.

10

The Bitter Taste of Regret

The door clicked softly as Adelaide left, her presence lingering like a bittersweet memory. I stood frozen for a moment, staring at the space she had just vacated, the air still heavy with the scent of her perfume. A familiar mix of roses and something sweet—lavender, perhaps. My hands trembled slightly as I reached for the back of my chair, steadying myself against the sudden wave of emotions that threatened to pull me under.

It wasn't just the scandal, the gossip, or even the accusations that cut me so deeply. It was the sight of Adelaide—six months pregnant, glowing with the life she carried inside her, and rubbing her swollen belly with the kind of affection that only a mother could have. The joy in her eyes, the happiness in her voice as she spoke of her unborn child—it broke something inside me.

With a heavy sigh, I turned toward the sideboard, my gaze falling on the crystal decanter that had been taunting me for what felt like hours. I hadn't touched a drop since the scandal broke, trying to keep a clear head, to face the disaster with the composure it demanded. But seeing Adelaide like that... it had cracked something open in me, something I'd been trying to bury for a long time.

The truth was, I didn't know where everything had gone wrong. Maybe it was the night I found myself in the arms of another woman at a ball, desperate to erase the feelings I had for Adelaide. The memory was still vivid, the way I had clung to that woman, hoping her lips would make me forget the way Adelaide's smile made my heart ache. I'd kissed her with a fervor that bordered on desperation, trying to drown out the longing that gnawed at me every time I saw Adelaide.

It hadn't worked. The woman had pulled away, confused by the intensity I couldn't explain. And afterward, as I watched her disappear into the crowd, I felt nothing but emptiness. But the impact was completely different, a few weeks later I saw Adelaide laughing with Duke Bastian, her eyes sparkling with a happiness that was never meant for me.

Or maybe it had gone wrong the day I realized too late that my feelings for Adelaide had only grown stronger over the years. By the time I knew what I wanted, she was already slipping through my fingers, falling into the arms of another man—another man who had made her happy in ways I never could.

Or perhaps it was when I failed to protect her. When the nobles turned against her, when the whispers and sneers had closed in around her like a tightening noose, I'd stood by, helpless, while she faced them alone. Duke Bastian had stepped in, had shielded her, had given her the strength to stand tall. Although Duke Bastian was also involved in the scandal, he took responsibility, apologized and took care of Adelaide. And I'd realized then that she was no longer mine to protect, if she ever had been.

I didn't know where it had all gone wrong, but the result was the same: I was too late. Adelaide was no longer possible. She was carrying another man's child, living another man's life, and all I could do was watch from the sidelines, drowning in regrets that I could never voice.

My hand shook as I poured the amber liquid into the glass, watching it swirl and catch the light. The bitter scent of the whiskey hit my nostrils, sharp and inviting, and I took a long, slow drink, letting it burn its way down my throat. The warmth spread through my chest, but it did nothing to dull the ache that had settled deep in my bones.

I took another drink, then another, each one doing little more than making the edges of the room blur. I didn't want to think anymore, didn't want to feel. But even as the alcohol began to take effect, numbing the sharpest edges of my pain, I knew it was a temporary reprieve. The reality would still be there, waiting for me, no matter how much I tried to escape it.

I don't know how long I stood there, staring into the empty glass, before I finally called out for Harris. The old butler appeared almost instantly, his footsteps soft and measured as he approached. He took one look at the glass in my hand, the empty bottle beside it, and his brow furrowed with concern.

"Is everything all right, my lord?" Harris asked, his voice gentle.

"No," I said flatly, my voice sounding hollow even to my own ears. "But I need your help, Harris. We need to clear Anne's name. We need a plan."

Harris nodded, his expression shifting to one of focused determination. "Of course, my lord. What do you have in mind?"

I set the glass down on the table, running a hand through my hair as I tried to pull my thoughts together. "First," I began, my voice steadier now, "we need to make it clear that nothing improper happened between Anne and me. We'll start with a statement—something formal, from the both of us, denying the rumors outright."

"Very well," Harris said, his tone supportive. "But will that be enough to sway public opinion?"

I shook my head. "No, probably not. But it's a start. The statement needs to be distributed to the key members of the ton—those who control the flow of information. We need to ensure that the right people hear it, those with influence who can help quash the rumors."

Harris nodded, already making mental notes. "And what about the more personal touch, my lord? Perhaps a gesture that shows there is no ill will between the families?"

I considered that for a moment. Harris was right—something more than just a statement was needed. "A public appearance," I said slowly, the idea taking shape in my mind. "I'll arrange to be seen with Anne, somewhere prominent, in full view of society. Something that shows we are still on good terms, that the rumors haven't driven a wedge between us."

Harris looked thoughtful. "Perhaps a charity event, my lord? Something that would allow you both to be seen as working together, for a common cause?"

"Yes," I agreed, the plan solidifying. "A charity event. I'll speak to Adelaide and Duke Bastian, see if they would be willing to host it. Their presence would lend credibility to the event and show that the families are united."

Harris nodded again, his expression approving. "An excellent idea, my lord. And what of the press? They've played a significant role in spreading the scandal."

"The press will be difficult," I admitted, rubbing my temples again as the headache threatened to return. "But we'll need to control the narrative. I'll arrange an exclusive interview with a reputable journalist, someone we can trust to tell our side of the story without twisting it. We'll focus on Anne's virtues, her contributions to society, and the absurdity of the rumors. If we can sway public opinion, we can start to turn the tide."

Harris stood silently for a moment, considering the plan. "It's ambitious, my lord, but it could work. We'll need to move quickly, though, before the scandal gains any more traction."

"I know," I said, the weight of it all pressing down on me. "But we have no choice. We need to clear Anne's name, no matter what it takes."

Harris nodded, his eyes filled with a mixture of concern and respect. "I'll make the necessary arrangements, my lord. And rest assured, I'll do everything in my power to see this through."

I watched as he turned to leave, feeling a small flicker of hope amidst the sea of despair that had engulfed me. The plan wasn't perfect, but it was something—a way forward, a way to make things right, or at least to start mending what had been broken.

But as the door closed behind Harris and I was left alone once more, I couldn't shake the feeling that no matter what I did, it wouldn't be enough to change the past. The regret, the what-ifs, the bitter realization that I had lost something precious before I even knew I wanted it—all of it lingered, heavy and unyielding.

And no amount of whiskey could drown that out.

11

Caught Between Scandal and Sacrifice

I was sitting in my room, staring blankly out the window as the last light of the day faded into the horizon. The news Adelaide had delivered still echoed in my mind, a jumble of confusion, disbelief, and growing anger. Colin would be responsible for clearing up the scandal surrounding us—he would make sure my name was restored to its former respectability—but he would not marry me.

My hand gripped the arm of the chair so tightly that my knuckles turned white. I had always known that Colin was honorable, that he would step up when needed, but I had also assumed that, in doing so, marriage would be the natural outcome. That had been the whole point of this carefully constructed plan, hadn't it? To force his hand, to secure my future in a way that kept me out of the clutches of men like Earl Eric Blackwood or, God forbid, Timothy Crawford.

But this? This was not part of the plan.

My mind was a whirlwind of conflicting emotions. Should I be relieved that Colin was at least trying to salvage my reputation? Angry that he hadn't taken the obvious next step? Or terrified that all my scheming had led me to this very moment, and it was all slipping through my fingers?

Before I could sort through the chaos in my head, the door to my room swung open, and my father strode in, his expression a stormy mix of fury and frustration. The Earl of Windermere was not a man who displayed his emotions often, but when he did, it was like standing in the path of a hurricane.

"Anne," he began without preamble, his voice tight with barely controlled anger, "I've just spoken with Adelaide. She tells me that Colin Ashford has refused to marry you."

I opened my mouth to respond, but he cut me off, pacing back and forth in front of my chair like a caged animal. "Do you have any idea what this means? Your name may be cleared, but the damage is already done! The scandal has tarnished our family's reputation, and your pride is irreparably wounded. How do you think this reflects on me, on your mother, on your sister? You're ruined, Anne!"

I flinched at his harsh words, but I forced myself to remain composed. I wasn't ruined—not yet. But I knew that this situation could still spiral out of control if I didn't manage it carefully.

"Father," I began, trying to keep my voice steady, "Colin is doing what he can to make things right. He's working to clear my name—"

"But he's not marrying you," my father snapped, whirling around to face me, his eyes blazing with fury. "Do you understand what that means? Your name may be cleared, but your prospects—your future—are destroyed. The ton will remember this scandal for years, and every time your name is mentioned, it will be with a shadow of disgrace."

I swallowed hard, knowing he was right. The damage had already been done, and while Colin's efforts might clean up some of the mess, it wouldn't erase the stain on my reputation. But I had hoped that marriage—forced or not—would provide a solution. I hadn't anticipated this outcome.

My father stopped pacing and fixed me with a cold, determined stare. "There is only one solution left, Anne. You will marry Earl Eric Blackwood."

The blood drained from my face as his words sank in. "No," I whispered, shaking my head in disbelief. "Father, you can't be serious. Earl Eric is a notorious rake, a man with a reputation for debauchery and scandal. You can't possibly expect me to marry him."

"Can't I?" he retorted, his tone harsh and unyielding. "You've left me with no other choice. If Colin Ashford won't take responsibility for you, then you'll marry a man who will. Earl Eric may be a rake, but he's also a man of influence and wealth. Marrying him would restore some semblance of dignity to this family, and it would prevent you from becoming a laughingstock."

I felt a wave of panic rising within me, but I forced it down, clinging to my composure. "I won't do it," I said, my voice trembling with anger. "I won't marry Earl Eric, not after everything I've done to avoid that fate. And if you think I'll go along with this just because you say so—"

"Then you'll marry Timothy Crawford," my father interrupted, his tone resolute. "A respectable widower, with a sizable estate and five sons who need a mother. He may be older, but he's a better option than living in disgrace."

The sheer audacity of his ultimatum sent a surge of rage through me, and I stood up, my hands clenched at my sides. "Why, Father? Why are you so determined to throw me to the wolves? Adelaide refused Timothy Crawford's proposal and escaped that trap, so why should I be forced into it? Why must I be the one to suffer for this scandal?"

My father's expression darkened, and he took a step toward me, his voice low and dangerous. "Adelaide was fortunate to find a man like Duke Bastian. You, on the other hand, have squandered your chances. You've brought shame to this family, Anne, and you will do whatever it takes to repair the damage. Whether you marry Earl Eric or Mr. Crawford, you will marry, and you will do so immediately."

I stood there, trembling with fury, my mind racing. This was not how it was supposed to be. This was not the future I had envisioned for myself. But as I stared into my father's hard, unforgiving eyes, I knew there was no reasoning with him. He had made up his mind, and he would see me married off to the first man who would have me, regardless of my feelings or my future.

Without another word, I turned on my heel and stormed out of the room, my heart pounding in my chest. I needed to get away, to clear my head, to think. But the further I walked, the more my thoughts spiraled out of control.

If Colin succeeded in clearing my name without marriage, then what would I do? Would I really be forced to marry one of those awful men just to salvage what was left of my reputation? The thought made my stomach turn, and I found myself climbing the stairs to my room, seeking the only refuge I had left.

Once inside, I slammed the door shut behind me and collapsed onto the bed, burying my face in the pillows. Hot, angry tears welled up in my eyes, but I refused to let them fall. I wouldn't cry, not now. Not when I needed to be strong, to think clearly.

But the truth was, I was scared. Scared that everything I had worked for, everything I had planned, was crumbling around me. Scared that I was losing control of my own life, my own future.

And most of all, scared that Colin would succeed in clearing my name without marriage, leaving me with no choice but to marry a man I despised.

I took a deep, shaky breath and sat up, wiping away the tears that threatened to spill over. I needed to think, to figure out my next move. Because if Colin could clear my name without marrying me, then I would have to take matters into my own hands.

But how? And at what cost?

12

The Faint Praise and False Promises

Days passed in a blur of anxiety and dread, each one stretching longer than the last. I found myself clinging to any scrap of news, any whisper that might hint at the state of the scandal that had so thoroughly upended my life. I'd spent countless hours by the window, watching the street below, straining to catch snippets of conversation from passersby or the occasional carriage that rolled by. But it wasn't until I overheard the servants talking in hushed tones that I realized things might be changing.

One afternoon, as I descended the grand staircase, I paused halfway down, my ears pricking up at the sound of two maids whispering at the bottom.

"Did you hear? They say the Marquess is making amends," one of the maids said, her voice filled with a mixture of curiosity and relief. "The scandal's dying down—at least that's what Lady Windermere told Cook."

"Indeed?" the other maid replied. "I heard he's been seen with Miss Blair, attending events, showing the ton there's nothing amiss."

I gripped the banister, my heart leaping at the words. Could it be true? Could Colin's efforts actually be working? Was the scandal finally beginning to subside? The thought should have brought me relief, but instead, it filled me with a strange mix of emotions—gratitude, frustration, and a gnawing sense of urgency.

If the scandal truly was fading, then my time was running out. The very plan I had set in motion was slipping through my fingers. I had expected Colin to marry me to resolve the issue, but now... now I had to face the reality that he might clear my name without a marriage proposal. And then what? Would I be left with no choice but to marry Earl Eric or, worse, Timothy Crawford?

No, I couldn't let that happen. I had to think of something, some way to turn this situation back in my favor.

But before I could devise a plan, my father summoned me to the drawing room. I knew what awaited me there, and the thought sent a shiver of dread down my spine. Earl Eric Blackwood had come to call, and I had no choice but to face him.

With a deep breath, I entered the room, my heart sinking as I saw Earl Eric standing by the fireplace, his tall, imposing figure dressed in impeccable attire. His appearance was as polished as ever—his dark hair neatly combed, his cravat tied perfectly, and his expression a mask of practiced elegance. But I knew better. I had heard the rumors, seen the whispers behind fans, and I was well aware of the reputation that lurked beneath that polished exterior.

"Miss Blair," he greeted me with a smooth, practiced smile as I curtsied, the corners of his mouth lifting just enough to be considered polite. "A pleasure to see you again."

"Earl Eric," I replied, my voice steady despite the turmoil churning within me. "Thank you for calling."

He stepped forward, taking my hand in his gloved one, his touch lingering a moment longer than necessary. "The pleasure is mine, I assure you."

I forced a smile, though the very act of it made my skin crawl. I had hoped to avoid this meeting altogether, but my father's insistence had left me with little choice. Earl Eric's eyes lingered on mine, and for a moment, I saw a flicker of something—something sly and calculating—beneath his veneer of civility. I knew his reputation well enough to recognize it for what it was: the charming predator, sizing up his prey.

But I was no innocent lamb. I had played this game before, and if Earl Eric wanted to charm me into submission, he would find himself sorely mistaken.

He led me to a settee near the window, guiding me to sit as if I were some fragile flower in need of protection. I kept my expression composed, my movements deliberate, as I arranged my skirts and folded my hands in my lap. I needed to buy time, to think, to figure out how to keep myself from being cornered into a marriage with this man.

"I must say," Earl Eric began, settling into the seat opposite me with an air of casual confidence, "you have borne the recent... unpleasantness with admirable grace, Miss Blair. It is not every young lady who can face such a trying time with such poise."

"Thank you," I replied, my voice cool and measured. "One must do what one can to navigate the challenges life presents."

His smile widened, and I could see the glint of something unsavory in his eyes. "Indeed. And I do believe that with the right support, those challenges can be overcome with ease. I am here to offer that support, Miss Blair—to see that you are well taken care of, that your good name is restored."

I resisted the urge to roll my eyes at his patronizing tone. "That is most generous of you, my lord."

"Oh, it is no trouble at all," he said, leaning in slightly, his voice dropping to a more intimate tone. "You see, I believe a woman of your beauty, your intelligence, deserves nothing less than to be cherished, to be admired and adored. I would be honored to offer you such a life, should you choose to accept it."

The words dripped with honey, but I could taste the poison beneath. I knew the kind of man Earl Eric was—the kind who whispered sweet promises in the dark, only to leave behind broken hearts and shattered reputations when morning came. The very thought of being tied to him made my stomach turn.

But I forced myself to smile, to play the game. "Your words are kind, my lord. However, I am still weighing my options, given the current situation."

His gaze darkened slightly, though the smile never left his face. "Of course, you must do what you feel is best. But time is of the essence, Miss Blair. The longer you wait, the more difficult it will be to repair the damage that has been done."

"I am aware," I replied, my tone even, though inside I seethed. He was pressing me, trying to corner me into a decision I wasn't ready to make. But I wouldn't let him rush me, not when there was still a chance—however slim—that I could find another way out of this mess.

Our conversation continued, a careful dance of words and smiles, each of us testing the other's resolve. Earl Eric was as charming as his reputation suggested, but I could see the impatience beneath his practiced demeanor. He wanted to secure the match, to bind me to him before I could find a way to escape.

But I wouldn't let him. Not yet. I needed more time to think, to plan, to figure out how to turn the situation back in my favor. Colin was still in London, still working to clear my name. If I could just find a way to tip the scales, to push him into a position where marriage was the only viable solution…

As our conversation drew to a close, I offered Earl Eric a polite but noncommittal response, thanking him for his visit and assuring him that I would consider his offer carefully. He left with a smile, but I could see the frustration in his eyes. He wasn't used to being kept waiting, and I knew it was only a matter of time before his patience wore thin.

But that was exactly what I needed—time. Time to think, time to plan, and time to find a way to ensure that Colin fell into the trap I had laid, before I was forced into a marriage that would trap me in a life of misery.

As I watched Earl Eric's carriage pull away from Windermere Manor, I felt the weight of my predicament settle over me like a suffocating shroud. The scandal might be subsiding, but the pressure was mounting, and I knew that my window of opportunity was closing fast.

But I wasn't beaten yet. I still had a few cards left to play, and I intended to play them to their fullest.

With a determined breath, I turned away from the window and made my way upstairs, my mind racing with possibilities. I needed to act quickly, to find a way to ensure that Colin couldn't simply walk away from this situation unscathed.

Because one thing was certain: I would not be marrying Earl Eric Blackwood. And I would do whatever it took to make sure that I was the one who controlled my own fate.

13

The Calm Before the Storm

The sun filtered through the tall windows of the drawing room, casting a warm glow over the tea party my mother had so meticulously arranged. The soft clinking of teacups, the rustling of silk gowns, and the gentle hum of conversation filled the room, creating a pleasant, almost serene atmosphere. But beneath the surface, I could feel the tension coiling in my chest, tightening with every word that was spoken.

I had been listening carefully to the noble ladies as they chatted with my mother, their voices light and airy, as if nothing in the world could disturb their delicate sensibilities. But the words they exchanged were far from idle gossip—they carried the weight of something far more significant.

"I must say," Lady Pembroke remarked with a smile, "it's such a relief that the unpleasantness surrounding your daughter has been resolved, Lady Windermere. We were all so concerned, but it seems the Marquess has handled the situation with great care."

My mother, always eager to bask in the praise of others, nodded graciously. "Yes, indeed. Colin has been most diligent in ensuring that Anne's reputation remains untarnished. It was all a terrible misunderstanding, of course, but these things can easily spiral out of control if not addressed promptly."

The words struck me like a blow, even though I had been expecting them. The scandal—the very one I had hoped would force Colin into marriage—had completely disappeared, erased from the minds of those who had once delighted in spreading it. Colin had succeeded in clearing my name, and while that should have been a cause for celebration, it left me feeling hollow inside.

"Colin's always been reliable," Adelaide chimed in, her tone full of admiration. She sat across from me, her hand resting protectively on her pregnant belly. "I never doubted him for a moment. I knew he would handle things with the utmost discretion and care. He's not the sort of man to make foolish decisions, after all."

I forced a smile, though it felt more like a grimace. Adelaide's words, spoken with such confidence and pride, only deepened the bitterness that gnawed at my insides. She had so much faith in Colin, so much trust in his judgment, and all I could think about was how completely my plan had backfired. The scandal had been my weapon, my means of securing my future, and now it was gone, leaving me with nothing but the prospect of a marriage I didn't want.

My mother, oblivious to my inner turmoil, continued the conversation with a smug smile. "And of course, we are most grateful to Earl Eric for his attentions to Anne during this trying time. He has been quite the gentleman, and I believe there is potential for something more serious between them."

The words made my stomach churn, but I kept my expression neutral, offering only a polite nod in response. The very idea of being tied to Earl Eric—of being forced into a marriage with a man I despised—was enough to make my blood run cold. And yet, my mother spoke of it as if it were a foregone conclusion, as if my fate had already been sealed.

"This is all such wonderful news," Lady Pembroke remarked, lifting her teacup to her lips. "A scandal averted, a promising courtship... It's a happy ending for everyone, it seems."

"Yes, everyone," I echoed softly, the bitterness creeping into my voice despite my efforts to keep it at bay.

Everyone except me. I glanced around the room, at the smiling faces of the noble ladies, at my mother's contented expression, at Adelaide's serene smile. They were all relieved, all pleased with the way things had turned out. But for me, the disappearance of the scandal was nothing short of a disaster.

Adelaide turned to me with a bright smile. "Oh, Anne, I nearly forgot to mention—Colin is organizing a charity event with the Lightwood family. He's been so busy with it, and I'm sure it will be a great success. You must come, of course. It will be a wonderful opportunity to show everyone that all is well."

The words were like a dagger to my heart. A charity event, organized by Colin, with the Lightwood family and other prominent families in attendance. It was the perfect setting, the perfect opportunity... and I knew, in that moment, what I had to do.

My smile widened, though it was devoid of any real warmth. "Of course, Adelaide. I wouldn't miss it for the world."

Adelaide beamed, clearly pleased with my response. But she had no idea what was brewing beneath the surface. None of them did. The scandal may have subsided, but I wasn't about to let it fade into obscurity. If Colin thought he could simply erase the past and move on, he was sorely mistaken.

As the tea party continued, I sat in silence, my mind racing with plans, with possibilities. I needed to make sure that the scandal didn't just resurface—it needed to explode. I needed to create a situation so undeniable, so outrageous, that not even Colin's meticulous efforts could undo it. This time, I wouldn't rely on whispers and rumors. This time, I would take matters into my own hands.

I would make sure that the scandal was talked about again, that it became so big, so unavoidable, that Colin—or even the Queen herself—couldn't erase it. And when that happened, there would be only one solution left.

As I sipped my tea, I allowed myself a small, satisfied smile. The game wasn't over—not by a long shot. I still had my cards to play, and I intended to play them to their fullest.

Because one thing was certain: I would not be marrying Earl Eric Blackwood. And I would do whatever it took to ensure that Colin Ashford had no choice but to marry me.

Let them think the storm had passed. They hadn't seen anything yet.

14

A Perfectly Orchestrated Disaster

Two weeks had passed since that fateful tea party, and I had spent every moment of them preparing for what was to come. I had pretended to be unwell, feigning fatigue and lethargy at every opportunity. My mother fussed over me, urging me to rest, to take care of myself, while I dutifully complied, hiding the true reason for my supposed ailment. My goal was to give the appearance of frailty, to gain just enough weight to make the illusion convincing when the time came.

Each day, I met with Earl Eric, ensuring that he—and by extension, society—had no reason to doubt my apparent weakness. I played the part of the demure, fragile woman, delicately sipping tea and speaking in soft, weary tones. But behind the scenes, I ate more than usual, carefully choosing foods that would cause me to bloat and gain a little weight. I needed just enough to create the illusion I had in mind, but not so much that anyone would suspect I was anything other than unwell.

The day of the charity event finally arrived, and I felt a knot of tension settle in my stomach as I dressed for the occasion. Today was the day everything would change, one way or another. The charity event was to be the grand culmination of Colin's efforts to restore our reputations, and the perfect stage for the final act of my plan.

Adelaide and Duke Bastian arrived at our home first, as was their custom whenever there was a grand event. Adelaide was radiant, her belly now noticeably round as she approached the final months of her pregnancy. She greeted me with a warm smile, clearly pleased to see me up and about after my supposed illness.

"Anne, you look better," she said with genuine relief, embracing me gently. "I was so worried about you."

I returned her embrace, careful not to let my own nerves show. "Thank you, Adelaide. I'm feeling much better today. I'm looking forward to the event."

As we gathered our things and prepared to leave, I felt the weight of what was to come pressing down on me. The charity event was the talk of the ton, a grand affair attended by the most prominent families in society. And at the center of it all was Colin, the man I had so carefully ensnared, the man who had nearly slipped through my grasp.

When we arrived at the venue, the sight that greeted us was as grand as I had expected. The ballroom was packed with elegantly dressed guests, the sound of conversation and laughter filling the air. Crystal chandeliers cast a warm, golden light over the scene, illuminating the glittering jewels and rich fabrics worn by the attendees. It was a picture of opulence and refinement, the very image of high society at its finest.

Colin was, as I had anticipated, the center of attention. He moved through the crowd with ease, his charm and charisma on full display as he greeted guests and accepted their praise for his contributions to the event. He looked every bit the perfect gentleman, his demeanor calm and composed, as if the scandal that had nearly ruined us both had never existed.

As we made our way into the ballroom, Adelaide and Duke Bastian by my side, I forced myself to remain composed. I couldn't afford to falter now, not when everything I had worked for was about to come to fruition.

We approached Colin, and he greeted us with a smile that didn't quite reach his eyes. There was a tension in his posture, a stiffness in his movements that told me he was still grappling with the events of the past month. He was trying to convince himself—and everyone else—that everything was fine, that the scandal had been nothing more than a momentary lapse of judgment, a misunderstanding blown out of proportion.

"Anne," he said, his voice smooth but with an edge of something darker beneath it. "It's good to see you here. You're looking well."

I smiled, allowing a hint of vulnerability to seep into my expression. "Thank you, Colin. I'm feeling much better, though I'm still not quite myself."

Adelaide beamed at him, clearly pleased by the interaction. "Colin, you've done a wonderful job with this event. It's exactly what we all needed to put the past behind us."

Colin's smile faltered for just a moment before he nodded. "Yes, I hope so. It was important to me that we all move forward."

But as he spoke, I noticed a figure approaching from across the room. Marquess Hawthorne, the owner of the manor where Colin and I had been found that fateful morning, was making his way toward us. This was the moment I had been waiting for, the moment when I would set the final piece of my plan into motion.

The marquess greeted us with a warm smile, his eyes lingering on me with what I could only describe as polite concern. "Miss Blair," he said, his voice full of genuine warmth, "it's so good to see you up and about. We were all so worried after your recent troubles."

And that was when I struck.

My hand went to my stomach, my expression shifting from one of polite composure to one of sudden distress. I covered my mouth with my other hand, as if trying to stifle a wave of nausea. "Oh," I gasped, my voice trembling as I clutched at my abdomen. "I... I think I—"

Before I could finish, I pretended to retch, a dry, choking sound that echoed through the ballroom. A ripple of shock went through the gathered guests, and I could feel all eyes turning toward me. The marquess reached out, his concern deepening. "Miss Blair, are you all right?"

Just as I had planned, Lady Eleanor Hawthorne appeared at my side, her face a mask of worry. She reached out to steady me, but I allowed myself to sway slightly, as if I might collapse at any moment. "I'm... I'm so sorry," I whispered, my voice breaking as I fought back tears. "I just... I feel so unwell..."

"Anne, what's wrong?" Adelaide asked, her voice filled with concern as she stepped forward.

I shook my head, my tears now genuine as the reality of what I was doing began to set in. "I... I don't know," I whispered, my voice trembling. "I've been feeling so ill for weeks now, and I just... I can't seem to get better..."

But the final blow came when I glanced up at Colin, my eyes meeting his as I let my expression crumble. I didn't need to say the words—my performance had already planted the seed of doubt in everyone's minds. The implications were clear, and the look on Colin's face told me that he understood exactly what I was insinuating.

He stood frozen in place, his face pale, his eyes wide with shock. The weight of what I was suggesting—what everyone in that room was now beginning to suspect—was crashing down on him, and for a moment, I saw something in his eyes that I had never seen before: fear.

Lady Eleanor took hold of my arm, her voice soft but insistent. "Miss Blair, you need to sit down. Let me help you—"

But as she spoke, the nausea I had been faking suddenly became all too real. I had eaten something particularly cloying that morning, a rich cream pastry that had left a sickly sweet taste in my mouth. The combination of nerves and the heavy food churned in my stomach, and before I could stop myself, I bolted for the door, my hand clamped over my mouth as I fought to hold back the inevitable.

I could hear the murmurs of the guests, the gasps of shock as I fled the ballroom, but all I could focus on was the overwhelming need to escape before I lost what little dignity I had left. My stomach roiled, and I barely made it outside before I was bent over, retching into the bushes.

I heard footsteps behind me, felt a gentle hand on my back, and knew it was Lady Eleanor who had followed me. "Anne, are you all right? Should I send for a physician?"

I shook my head, tears streaming down my face as I struggled to compose myself. "I... I'm fine," I choked out, though it was clear to both of us that I was anything but. "I just... need a moment."

As I leaned against the cool stone wall, trying to regain my breath, I knew that my plan had worked. The scandal would explode again, just as I had intended. And this time, it would be even bigger, even more undeniable than before.

Colin wouldn't be able to erase this. He wouldn't be able to escape the consequences. And neither would I.

15

The Unraveling

The aftermath of my dramatic exit from the charity ball unfolded exactly as I had hoped. Lady Eleanor Hawthorne had chased after me, her concern genuine as she helped me regain my composure in a secluded alcove just outside the ballroom. I had feigned weakness, leaning heavily on her arm as we returned to the gathering, every eye in the room fixed on me with a mixture of shock and suspicion.

But the true drama was yet to come.

As Lady Eleanor guided me back into the ballroom, the crowd parted like the Red Sea, whispers and gasps rippling through the throng of high society. The tension was palpable, the air thick with unspoken questions. What had just happened? Was it true? The rumors they had so gleefully dismissed just days before were now reignited, fanned into a blaze by my carefully executed performance.

Adelaide rushed to my side, her face pale with worry. "Anne, are you all right?" she asked, her voice trembling as she took my hand. "You look dreadful. We should take you home."

But I shook my head weakly, playing my part to perfection. "No, Adelaide, I... I don't want to cause a scene."

It was too late for that, of course. The scene had already been set, the actors in place, and the audience captivated by the unfolding drama. Colin stood frozen a few feet away, his face ashen, his eyes wide with disbelief. He looked like a man who had just been condemned, and in many ways, he had been.

Before anyone could take further action, Marquess Hawthorne appeared, his expression one of grave concern. "Miss Blair," he said, his voice steady and authoritative, "I think it's best we have a physician examine you immediately. We cannot take any risks with your health."

The room seemed to hold its collective breath, and I knew there was no turning back now. I nodded meekly, allowing myself to be led to a nearby room just off the main ballroom. The physician, the very one I had bribed to corroborate my story, was summoned with the utmost urgency. Within minutes, he arrived, his face a mask of professional concern as he carried his black bag into the room.

My family—along with Adelaide, Duke Bastian, Colin, and the Marquess—were all present. They watched in tense silence as the physician conducted his examination, each of them wearing an expression of anxious anticipation. I lay back on the chaise, my heart pounding, though not from fear. No, this was the thrill of knowing that I was moments away from sealing my fate—and Colin's.

The physician, as planned, took his time, his movements deliberate and careful as he examined me. He asked a few questions, to which I responded with feigned frailty, doing everything in my power to maintain the illusion of a woman in delicate condition. Every so often, I caught Colin's eye, watching as the dawning horror etched itself deeper into his features.

Finally, the physician straightened, his expression solemn as he turned to address the room. "My lord," he began, addressing my father directly, "after a thorough examination, I must inform you that Miss Blair is most likely pregnant—approximately four weeks along."

A collective gasp went up around the room, my mother's hand flying to her mouth in shock. Adelaide's eyes widened, while Duke Bastian looked between Colin and me with a deepening frown. The Marquess exchanged a grim glance with the physician, as if the two of them had just confirmed something they had both feared.

But it was Colin's reaction that I had been waiting for. His face turned as white as a sheet, his body rigid with tension as the reality of the situation sank in. He opened his mouth as if to speak, but no words came out. The truth—or rather, the carefully constructed lie—was now out in the open, and there was no escaping it.

Marquess Hawthorne cleared his throat, stepping forward to address my family. "Lord Windermere, Lady Windermere, I must express my deepest regrets for what has transpired. As you know, the morning after the incident at my manor, both Colin and Miss Blair were discovered... in a compromising situation. They were found unclothed and asleep together, and while I initially believed it to be a misunderstanding, it seems that the consequences of that night have been more serious than we realized."

He turned to my parents, bowing his head in contrition. "I apologize for my role in this unfortunate situation. Had I been more vigilant, perhaps we could have avoided this outcome."

My father's face was a storm of fury, his eyes blazing with barely contained rage. "This is an outrage," he spat, his voice low and dangerous. "My daughter's reputation—our family's honor—has been dragged through the mud, and now you tell me she is with child?"

The physician remained calm, his gaze steady as he nodded. "I understand your distress, my lord, but the evidence is clear. Miss Blair is indeed pregnant, and given the timing, it is highly likely that the conception occurred around the time of the incident."

The room fell into a heavy silence, the implications of the physician's words settling over us like a suffocating shroud. This was it. The final blow. There would be no turning back now, no way for Colin to extricate himself from the trap I had so carefully set.

Colin looked at me, his eyes filled with a mix of shock and despair. "Anne... is this true?" he whispered, his voice barely audible.

I met his gaze, allowing my eyes to brim with tears, my voice trembling with a mixture of sorrow and determination. "Colin, I never wanted this," I whispered, loud enough for everyone in the room to hear. "I never wanted to trap you, to force you into something you didn't want. But now... now there's no choice."

The room remained deathly silent as my words hung in the air. I could see the realization dawning on Colin, the understanding that his life—our lives—had been irrevocably altered by the events of that night. He was trapped, just as I had planned, and there was no escape.

Finally, my father spoke, his voice laced with cold finality. "There is only one honorable course of action left, Colin. You will marry my daughter and do right by her and this family."

Colin's shoulders sagged, the weight of the situation pressing down on him from all sides. He nodded slowly, his expression one of resigned defeat. "Yes, my lord," he said quietly, his voice barely above a whisper. "I will take responsibility."

As I lay there, surrounded by the people who believed they knew the truth, I allowed myself a small, secret smile. The plan had worked. The scandal would explode once more, and this time, there would be no escape for Colin.

Our fates were now intertwined, bound by the lies I had so carefully spun. And while the cost had been great, I had secured my future—at least for now.

16

Shattered Trust

The room spun around me, a blur of colors and sounds that I could barely register. Anne's words echoed in my mind, their implications crashing over me like a tidal wave. Pregnant. Anne was pregnant, and the child was supposedly mine. The shock was paralyzing, a cold, suffocating dread that wrapped itself around my chest and squeezed until I could hardly breathe.

How had it come to this? How had everything gone so disastrously wrong?

I felt my knees weaken as the reality of the situation sank in. The scandal that I had worked so hard to suppress, to erase, had now grown into something far more destructive. And now, with Anne's pregnancy, there was no escape. The trap had closed around me, and I had no way out.

Before I could even begin to process what had just happened, I heard Adelaide's voice, sharp and cutting through the fog in my mind. She was standing just a few feet away, her expression one of betrayal and anger. Her eyes, usually so warm and full of trust, were now filled with a pain that cut me to the core.

"Colin," she hissed, her voice trembling with rage. "How could you? How could you do this to my sister?"

I opened my mouth to respond, to explain, to defend myself, but the words wouldn't come. What could I say? How could I possibly explain something that I didn't even understand myself? All I knew was that my life was unraveling before my eyes, and I was powerless to stop it.

Adelaide took a step closer, her hands clenched into fists at her sides. "I believed in you, Colin. I trusted you. I thought you were better than this—better than the rumors, better than the lies. But now... now I see I was wrong."

Each word was a dagger, piercing straight through me, leaving a wound that bled with guilt and shame. Adelaide had always been the one who believed in me, who saw the best in me even when I couldn't see it myself. And now, that belief was gone, shattered by the reality of what I had supposedly done.

"Why, Colin?" she demanded, her voice breaking as she fought back tears. "Why did you do this? Why did you betray us like this?"

I couldn't answer. I had no defense, no explanation that could make sense of the situation. All I could do was stand there, silent and stricken, as Adelaide's anger and hurt washed over me.

I felt something break inside me, a piece of myself that had held on to the hope that somehow, this would all work out, that the scandal could be contained, that I could still be the man Adelaide believed I was. But now, that hope was gone, crushed beneath the weight of the accusations that I couldn't deny.

Just as Adelaide seemed ready to unleash another round of accusations, I saw her face suddenly go pale, her eyes widening in alarm. Her hands instinctively went to her belly, cradling the seven-month swell of her pregnancy as she swayed on her feet.

"Adelaide!" I cried out, my shock momentarily forgotten as I rushed forward to catch her before she fell. My arms went around her, steadying her as she leaned heavily against me, her breath coming in shallow gasps.

Duke Bastian was at her side in an instant, his face a mask of concern and barely suppressed anger. He practically shoved me aside as he lifted Adelaide into his arms, cradling her as if she were made of glass. I stepped back, my heart pounding in my chest, feeling utterly helpless as I watched the man I had always respected carry his wife to the nearest sofa.

"Get the physician," Bastian ordered, his voice sharp and commanding.

The physician, who had just delivered the devastating news of Anne's pregnancy, was quick to respond, moving to Adelaide's side with practiced efficiency. The tension in the room was palpable as he examined her, his brow furrowing in concentration.

I stood frozen, my thoughts a chaotic jumble of guilt, fear, and despair. The sight of Adelaide lying there, her usually vibrant face now pale and drawn, filled me with a wave of dread that nearly brought me to my knees. The baby—her baby—was my responsibility too, in a way that went beyond mere friendship. I had promised to protect Adelaide, to look out for her, and now... now I had failed her in the worst possible way.

When the physician finally straightened, his expression was serious but not panicked. "The stress of the situation has caused a bit of strain, but the Duchess and the baby are both fine. She just needs to rest, to avoid any more excitement."

Bastian nodded, his face still tight with worry as he gently smoothed Adelaide's hair back from her face. She was breathing more evenly now, her eyes closed as she lay there, but the tension in her body hadn't entirely eased.

As the physician gave his diagnosis, I felt a deep, gnawing sense of guilt settle in the pit of my stomach. This was all my fault. If I hadn't been so blind, so careless, none of this would have happened. Adelaide wouldn't be lying there, her health compromised by the very scandal I had been trying to avoid.

And then my thoughts turned to Anne. How had it come to this? Out of all the women in England, why did it have to be Anne—Adelaide's sister, Duke Bastian's sister-in-law? She had been caught in this web of scandal because of me, and now her life was in ruins. I had dragged her into a nightmare, one that I couldn't wake us from.

Anne had always been kind, sharp-minded, someone I respected and admired. She deserved better than this. Better than to be the subject of cruel gossip, better than to be the one bearing the weight of this terrible mistake. I wanted to apologize, to fall on my knees and beg her forgiveness for the mess I had made of her life.

The room was filled with a heavy silence as we all absorbed the gravity of the situation. My world had come crashing down around me, and there was no way to fix it, no way to turn back the clock and undo the damage that had been done.

I had lost Adelaide's trust, shattered whatever respect Bastian had for me, and now I was bound to a future I hadn't chosen—one that had been thrust upon me by my own foolish actions.

I was trapped, and there was no way out.

17

A Hollow Promise

The room felt suffocating as Duke Bastian lifted Adelaide into his arms, her head resting weakly against his shoulder. He didn't say a word, his face a mask of carefully controlled emotion, as he turned and carried her out of the room. The weight of the unspoken words between us hung heavily in the air, but I couldn't muster the strength to speak. My throat was tight with guilt, shame, and a deep, gnawing regret that I couldn't shake.

No one questioned Bastian's abrupt departure, not with Adelaide so clearly unwell. We all watched as he left, his protective grip on her making it clear that nothing else mattered to him in that moment but his wife and unborn child.

I couldn't tear my eyes away from Adelaide's belly, so prominently rounded with the life growing inside her. The child that should have been mine. The future I had once imagined, now so far out of reach it felt like a cruel joke. My heart twisted with a bitter envy, knowing that Bastian had everything I had once dreamed of—Adelaide's love, her trust, her future.

And then there was Anne, who stood quietly across the room, the very picture of fragility. The woman carrying my child. A child I hadn't expected, hadn't wanted, and yet, it was mine nonetheless. The cruel irony of the situation hit me like a punch to the gut. The woman I had once considered as nothing more than a sister-in-law to my best friend now bore the weight of my mistakes.

As the last of the guests filtered out, leaving us alone, the silence grew thick between us. I stood there, rooted to the spot, unsure of how to begin, what to say, or how to apologize for something so monumental, so life-altering. The words stuck in my throat, choking me with their enormity.

Finally, unable to hold back the crushing guilt any longer, I dropped to my knees before her, my hands clenched into fists on the floor. I couldn't look her in the eye. "Anne," I began, my voice hoarse with emotion, "I am so sorry. I never wanted this—for you, for me, for any of us. I've been a fool, and I've let you suffer alone with... with our child. I swear to you, I'll take responsibility. I'll make this right, somehow."

The weight of those words nearly crushed me. I had no idea how to make things right, no idea what the future would look like, but there was no escaping the fact that I had to try.

Anne remained silent for a long moment, and I dared to look up at her, my heart pounding in my chest. Her face was pale, her expression unreadable, but there was a glint of something in her eyes—something that told me she had already made her decision, long before this moment.

"Colin," she finally said, her voice soft and tinged with a weariness that matched my own. "I don't want a grand wedding. I've been embarrassed enough by the scandal, and I don't want to draw any more attention to us than necessary. We need to marry before... before my condition becomes obvious."

I nodded, feeling a lump form in my throat. "Of course. We'll have a simple wedding, just the two of us and a few witnesses. Whatever you want, Anne. I just want to do right by you."

Her gaze softened slightly, and she sighed, her shoulders slumping as if the weight of the world had settled upon them. "Adelaide's belly was quite noticeable when she was only eight weeks along," she murmured, almost to herself. "I'm sure I'll be the same. We have less than a month, Colin. We need to act quickly."

Less than a month. The timeline felt impossibly short, as if my entire life was hurtling toward an inevitable conclusion that I couldn't escape. I had once thought I had all the time in the world to make decisions, to shape my future, but now... now time was slipping through my fingers like sand.

"I'll make the arrangements," I promised, my voice thick with the weight of responsibility. "We'll be married within the week."

Anne nodded, a small, resigned smile tugging at her lips. There was no joy in her expression, no excitement for what was to come. Only acceptance. Acceptance of the reality that we were both trapped in, a reality that neither of us had chosen but one we now had to face together.

I wanted to reach out to her, to offer some kind of comfort, but the distance between us felt insurmountable. The gulf that had opened up between us in the wake of the scandal was too wide, too deep to bridge with words or gestures. I had never felt so helpless, so lost in my entire life.

As I rose to my feet, I realized that the future ahead of us was not the one I had ever imagined, and it certainly wasn't the one I wanted. But it was the one I had to live with. I had made my bed, and now I would lie in it—alongside the woman carrying my child, a woman I barely knew but was now bound to for life.

The air between us was thick with unspoken words, and as I turned to leave, I couldn't shake the feeling that I had lost something precious, something irreplaceable. Not just the future I had once dreamed of with Adelaide, but a part of myself that I could never reclaim.

The door closed behind me with a soft click, but the sound echoed in my mind like a final, irrevocable sentence.

There was no turning back now.

18

The Price of Deceit

The chaos that had erupted because of my actions had left me shaken, especially when Adelaide fainted. For a moment, I had feared that everything would unravel, that my carefully laid plans would crumble. But as the panic settled, I saw that my trap had sprung perfectly.

Colin, visibly distraught, had turned to my family, his voice thick with guilt and resignation. "I'll marry Anne," he said, the words sounding like they were torn from him. "We'll marry within the week. I... I'm sorry it won't be the wedding she deserves, but there's no time for anything grand. I can't risk her being exhausted, or... or anything happening to the baby."

My father's expression hardened, disappointment etched deep into the lines of his face. He looked at Colin for a long moment, the weight of the situation pressing down on all of us. "Very well," he finally said, his voice heavy. "We'll make the necessary arrangements."

The ride home was a silent one, the air thick with tension. My father hadn't spoken another word, his disapproval palpable. My mother sat beside me, her hands folded tightly in her lap, her eyes fixed on the passing landscape. I could feel the disappointment radiating from both of them, and it cut deeper than I had anticipated. But I couldn't afford to let it sway me. I had made my choice, and I had to see it through.

When we arrived home, my father barely waited for the carriage to stop before stepping out, his expression still unreadable. As I moved to follow, I felt my mother's hand on my arm, holding me back. "Come with me, Anne," she said softly, her voice laced with an emotion I couldn't quite place.

She led me upstairs, guiding me into my room and closing the door behind us. For a moment, she simply looked at me, her eyes searching mine as if trying to understand the daughter standing before her.

"Anne," she began, her voice trembling slightly, "I know... I know things have not turned out the way you imagined. I can see that you're frightened, and I'm sure this isn't what you wanted."

I felt a lump form in my throat, her empathy catching me off guard. "Mother, I..."

She shook her head, cutting off my words. "Let me finish, darling," she said gently, reaching out to take my hands in hers. "You're my daughter, Anne. And you're going to have a baby—a child who will need you to be strong, to be resilient. I want you to know that I'm here for you, no matter what. I may not understand everything you've done, but I love you, and I want to help you through this."

Her words were a balm to my frayed nerves, and I felt tears sting my eyes. I hadn't expected her to be so understanding, to offer me support when I had been bracing myself for condemnation. It was almost too much, and I had to swallow back the urge to confess everything, to unburden myself of the guilt that had been gnawing at me.

But I couldn't. Not now.

Instead, I forced a small, strained smile. "Thank you, Mother," I whispered. "I... I'm sorry for the trouble I've caused."

She pulled me into a gentle embrace, her arms warm and comforting around me. "It's all right, Anne," she murmured. "We'll get through this together. I just want you to focus on taking care of yourself and the baby."

When she finally released me, I felt a mix of relief and lingering guilt. But there was no turning back now. The plan was in motion, and I had to see it through, no matter the cost.

After my mother left, I sat on the edge of my bed, the weight of the day's events pressing down on me. Colin had agreed to marry me within the week, and now all I had to do was ensure that nothing went wrong before the wedding. There was no room for error, no time for second thoughts.

I glanced out the window at the darkening sky, a small, determined smile tugging at my lips. I had come this far, and I wouldn't let anything—or anyone—stand in my way. Not now. Not when the future I had fought so hard to secure was finally within my grasp.

This week, I would marry Colin Ashford. And I would make sure nothing derailed my carefully laid plans.

19

The Burdens and Boundaries

The days after my conversation with Anne passed in a blur of strained silence and heavy expectations. I had given my word that I would marry her, and now all that remained was to endure the days leading up to the wedding. My mind was a tangle of conflicting emotions—regret, resignation, and a deep-seated weariness that seemed to settle into my bones.

I was in my study, staring blankly at a stack of papers that required my attention, when the butler announced Duke Bastian's arrival. The news caught me off guard. Bastian, for all his power and influence, was not a man who visited without a clear purpose. His presence here, at Ashford Manor, could only mean one thing: this visit was about Anne.

I rose to greet him, adopting the practiced civility that men of our rank were expected to maintain. "Your Grace," I said, bowing slightly as he entered the room. "To what do I owe the pleasure of your visit?"

Bastian wasted no time with pleasantries. "I've come to discuss about Anne," he said, his tone as direct as his gaze. "You're to marry her as soon as possible."

I stiffened at the bluntness of his statement, though I shouldn't have been surprised. Bastian had always been a man who valued efficiency, who preferred to get straight to the point. "I've already agreed to marry her," I replied evenly. "The arrangements are being made."

Bastian nodded, but there was no relief in his expression. Instead, his eyes bore into mine with an intensity that left no room for misunderstanding. "I know this isn't the match you wanted, Colin. But Anne is my wife's sister, and the child she carries is my future nephew or niece. I expect you to make her happy."

There was a weight to his words, a seriousness that made it clear this was more than a simple request. It was an expectation, one that I had no choice but to fulfill. But something in his tone made me pause, and I found myself asking, "Why now, Yoru Grace? Why intervene now, when you've never involved yourself in such matters before?"

Bastian's expression hardened, his gaze narrowing slightly. "Because Anne is family. And because Adelaide has been sick with worry over this... drama you and Anne have created." His voice carried a subtle edge, a warning that I would do well to heed. "I won't have her health compromised further."

I nodded, feeling the weight of his words settle over me like a shroud. The last thing I wanted was to cause more harm, especially to Adelaide, whose well-being had always been a priority for me. But there was something else in Bastian's demeanor, something that made the hairs on the back of my neck stand on end.

Bastian took a step closer, his voice lowering as he spoke. "Colin, I'll be blunt. I've noticed the way you look at Adelaide. It needs to stop. She's my wife, and I don't appreciate it. Adelaide is mine."

The words hit me like a physical blow, and I clenched my fists at my sides, a surge of anger rising in my chest. How dare he? I had never crossed that line, had never acted on the feelings I'd buried so deeply. But Bastian's insinuation, his warning, stung more than I cared to admit.

My jaw tightened as I struggled to keep my composure. "You're very fortunate, Your Grace," I said, my voice low and strained. "You managed to secure Adelaide's hand using the same scandalous tactics that have ensnared me now."

Bastian's expression didn't change, but there was a flicker of something in his eyes—a hint of cold amusement. "Perhaps," he replied, his tone almost dismissive. "But I would have had Adelaide with or without the scandal. She was always meant to be mine."

The finality of his words hung in the air like a guillotine's blade, sharp and inevitable. He smiled faintly, a smile that held no warmth, no camaraderie. It was a smile that told me he had already won, and there was nothing I could do to change that.

Before I could respond, Bastian turned and walked away, leaving the room with the same unhurried confidence he had entered with. As the door closed behind him, I felt a rush of frustration and helplessness, my fists still clenched at my sides. Bastian's warning echoed in my mind, mingling with the resentment that simmered just beneath the surface.

I had been trapped by circumstances beyond my control, and now I was bound to a future I hadn't chosen, with a woman I hadn't wanted. But the most painful truth of all was that Bastian had what I could never have—Adelaide's love, her loyalty, her future.

I took a deep breath, forcing myself to release the tension in my body. The anger, the bitterness, it would do me no good. I had made my choices, or rather, the choices had been made for me, and now I had to live with the consequences.

As I returned to my desk, I tried to focus on the tasks before me, but my thoughts kept drifting back to Bastian's words, to the cold certainty in his voice. He had everything I wanted, and yet, he had the audacity to warn me off.

The unfairness of it all gnawed at me, but there was nothing I could do. I was trapped—trapped in a life that was no longer my own.

And all I could do was hope that somehow, some way, I could find a way to live with it.

20

The Unsettling Union

The day of the wedding had finally arrived, a day I had both dreaded and anticipated in equal measure. The preparations had been swift, almost hurried, but everything had come together as planned. A day that should have been filled with joy and celebration, but instead was shrouded in tension and unspoken regret. The ceremony was small and private, a necessity to keep Adelaide's mind at ease during her pregnancy. The last thing anyone wanted was for her to be further distressed by the scandal that had forced this union.

As I stood in front of the mirror, the weight of everything I had done pressed down on me like a suffocating blanket. The reflection that stared back at me was a woman dressed in a gown of ivory silk and delicate lace, her beauty meticulously crafted by skilled hands. But beneath the surface, I was a mess of conflicting emotions—guilt, fear, and a deep sense of foreboding that refused to be ignored.

Adelaide hovered nearby, her face glowing with the radiance of impending motherhood. She complimented me repeatedly, her voice filled with genuine warmth. "Anne, you look absolutely stunning. Colin won't be able to take his eyes off you."

I forced a smile, nodding in acknowledgment of her words. Adelaide's happiness, her unwavering support, only made the weight on my conscience heavier. How could she be so kind, so loving, when I had dragged her and everyone else into this mess? But I couldn't dwell on that now. The die was cast, and I had to see it through.

My mother fussed over me, her concern evident in the way she adjusted my veil and smoothed the fabric of my dress. "Are you sure you're comfortable, dear? Is your stomach hurting at all?"

I gently rubbed my belly, offering her a smile that I hoped was reassuring. "The baby is fine, Mother," I said softly. "Everything's going to be fine."

The maid who had helped me into the wedding dress had been exceedingly careful, her hands gentle as she fastened the intricate buttons and adjusted the lace. The dress was beautiful, a vision of luxury and elegance, despite the simplicity of the ceremony. But as I stood there, wrapped in the finest silk, I couldn't shake the feeling that this gown was less a garment of celebration and more a shroud, binding me to a future I wasn't sure I wanted.

The ceremony itself was held in the small chapel at Ashford Manor, with only the closest family and a few select guests in attendance. The air was thick with the murmur of whispered conversations as I was escorted to the altar, my heart pounding in my chest with each step. It was a beautiful ceremony, yes, but the atmosphere was anything but joyous.

Colin stood waiting for me, his expression a mask of calm determination. He looked every bit the perfect groom, his posture straight, his eyes focused on me as I approached. But I could see the tension in his jaw, the subtle tightness around his eyes. This was not a union born of love or desire, but one forged out of necessity, out of the consequences of our actions.

There was a palpable strain between us, a sense of distance that had nothing to do with physical space. I knew that Colin was going through the motions out of a sense of duty, not joy. He had been forced into this, just as much as I had forced myself into it, and the knowledge of that gnawed at me, filling me with a deep, unshakable guilt.

The vows were spoken with quiet solemnity, each word a binding thread that tied us together in the eyes of God and society. I recited the promises with as much sincerity as I could muster, my voice steady even as my mind raced. This was it. This was the moment that would seal my fate, that would bind me to Colin for the rest of our lives.

But then, just as Colin was about to slip the ring onto my finger, it happened. The ring—a delicate band of gold—slipped from his grasp and tumbled to the floor. It rolled across the polished stone, skittering away from us and coming to rest at the feet of one of the guests. A hush fell over the room, the sound of the ring's journey echoing in the silence.

My breath caught in my throat as I watched the ring disappear from sight, a small, seemingly inconsequential accident that nevertheless sent a shiver of unease down my spine. I stood frozen, my hand still outstretched, as if time itself had paused in that moment.

And then, Earl Eric Blackwood bent down to retrieve the ring.

He straightened, holding the ring between his fingers with a smile that didn't quite reach his eyes. There was something in his gaze, something dark and calculating, as he handed the ring back to Colin. "You seem to have dropped this," he said, his voice smooth and untroubled. But there was a glint in his eyes that made my skin crawl, a hint of something malevolent lurking beneath the surface.

"Thank you," Colin replied, his voice steady but devoid of warmth. He took the ring from Earl Eric's hand, his movements precise as he finally placed it on my finger.

But the chill that had settled in my bones refused to dissipate. I glanced at Earl Eric, only to find him watching us with that same unnerving smile. It might have been nothing, just a coincidental mishap, but the look in his eyes told me otherwise. It was as if he knew something, as if he held some secret knowledge that would unravel everything I had worked so hard to achieve.

I quickly looked away, forcing myself to focus on the ceremony, to block out the disquieting thoughts that threatened to overtake me. This was not the time for doubts, for second-guessing the decisions that had led me here. I had to stay focused, to see this through to the end.

Despite the slight incident, the wedding proceeded without further interruption. Colin and I exchanged the final vows, and as the priest pronounced us husband and wife, Colin leaned in to kiss me. The kiss was brief, perfunctory, a mere formality to seal the union. There was no passion, no tenderness—only the cold reality of the situation we had both found ourselves in.

THE UNSETTLING UNION

As we turned to face the small gathering of guests, I forced another smile, one that barely concealed the turmoil churning beneath the surface. The ceremony had ended, and I was now Lady Ashford, Colin's wife. The trap I had set had worked, and yet, as I looked out at the faces of those gathered to witness our union, I couldn't shake the feeling that something was amiss, that the consequences of my actions had only just begun to unfold.

The guests offered their polite congratulations, their expressions carefully neutral as they assessed the situation. No one openly questioned the circumstances, but I could see the curiosity in their eyes, the unspoken questions that would no doubt fuel the gossip in the days to come.

As Colin and I walked down the aisle, arm in arm, I stole a glance at him. His face was a mask, betraying none of the emotions I knew must be roiling within him. He was resigned, accepting of the path we had been forced to take, but there was no joy in his eyes, no warmth in his touch.

And as we exited the chapel, the weight of my decisions pressed down on me more heavily than ever. The wedding was over, and now we had to face the reality of the life we had bound ourselves to.

I was Lady Ashford, yes. But at what cost? And what new challenges lay ahead, waiting to test the fragile foundation of our marriage?

Only time would tell.

21

A Heavy Band

The weight of the ring on my finger felt foreign, heavy, as if it didn't belong. And in a way, it didn't. The wedding band represented a life I hadn't chosen, a future I had been forced into by circumstances beyond my control. I twisted the ring absently as the carriage rumbled along the road to Ashford Manor, my gaze shifting between the band of gold and the passing scenery outside the window.

I was married. The words echoed in my mind, yet they didn't seem real. The ceremony had passed in a blur, a series of motions that I had gone through with the detachment of a man walking to the gallows. I had said the vows, placed the ring on Anne's finger, and kissed her to seal the union, but my heart had been elsewhere, lost in the chaos of emotions that churned within me.

Anne sat beside me in the carriage, her posture stiff, her hands clasped tightly in her lap. She hadn't said much since we left the chapel, and the silence between us was thick with unspoken thoughts. I stole a glance at her, wondering if her mind was as frantic as mine. Her face was calm, composed, but I knew her well enough to see the tension in the set of her jaw, the way her eyes remained fixed on the space in front of her, unseeing.

Neither of us spoke, and I found myself grateful for the quiet. I didn't know what to say, didn't have the words to bridge the chasm that had opened between us. What was there to say, after all? We were both trapped in this marriage, bound by duty and obligation rather than love or desire. What could I possibly offer her that wouldn't sound hollow or insincere?

The ring twisted again on my finger, a constant reminder of the reality I had to face. I had never imagined that this would be my future, that I would be married to Anne Blair out of necessity, with the shadow of a scandal hanging over us like a dark cloud. And yet, here I was, bound to her by vows spoken before God and society, with no way to undo what had been done.

The carriage finally pulled up to Ashford Manor, and I felt a strange mix of relief and dread settle over me. This was my home, the place where I had always felt most at ease, but now it felt different—like a prison I had unwittingly stepped into. As we disembarked, the staff was already lined up, ready to greet their new mistress. They bowed and curtsied, their expressions carefully neutral, but I could see the curiosity in their eyes, the way they assessed Anne as she was introduced as the new hostess.

I walked beside her, going through the formalities with the same detached calm I had displayed throughout the day. "This is your home now," I said, the words sounding more like a formality than a genuine welcome. "If there's anything you need, the staff will see to it."

Anne nodded, offering a polite smile to the assembled servants. "Thank you," she replied, her voice steady, though I could sense the underlying tension in her tone.

Once the introductions were over, I escorted Anne to her room—a room that would now be hers alone, separate from mine. The silence between us stretched on as we walked, neither of us knowing what to say. When we reached her door, I hesitated for a moment, searching for the right words, but finding none that felt appropriate.

"You should rest," I finally said, my voice sounding more distant than I intended. "It's been a long day."

Anne looked at me, her eyes searching mine as if trying to read my thoughts. I wondered if she could see the turmoil within me, the guilt and regret that I couldn't quite hide. "Yes, it has," she agreed softly, her voice barely above a whisper.

There was a brief, awkward pause as we stood there, both of us knowing that we were supposed to say something more, something that would acknowledge the reality of our new life together. But the words wouldn't come, and the silence between us grew heavier by the second.

Finally, I nodded, forcing a semblance of a smile. "Goodnight, Anne."

"Goodnight, Colin," she replied, her voice tinged with an emotion I couldn't quite place.

Without another word, I turned and walked away, leaving her standing in the doorway. My steps were quick, purposeful, driven by the need to escape the weight of her gaze, the unspoken questions in her eyes. I couldn't bear to linger, to confront the reality of our situation any longer than necessary.

As I made my way to my own chambers, I couldn't shake the feeling of unease that had settled over me. The marriage was real, the vows binding, but everything about it felt wrong, like a poorly fitted suit that chafed and pinched at every turn. The ring on my finger was a constant reminder of the life I was now bound to, a life that I hadn't chosen but one I had to live nonetheless.

I closed the door to my room behind me, leaning against it for a moment as I let out a heavy breath. The day was over, but the reality of my new life had only just begun. And as I stood there, staring at the empty space around me, I couldn't help but wonder how long it would be before the weight of it all became too much to bear.

22

A Game of Patience

Three days had passed since our wedding, and I found myself in a curious state of contentment, though not without a lingering sense of unease. The marriage to Colin had been consummated in the most basic sense—we were bound by vows, living under the same roof, and going through the motions of a married couple. But the deeper connection, the intimacy that should have followed, remained elusive.

Despite everything, I had to admit that life as the Marchioness of Ashford was not without its comforts. Colin, though distant, was kind and well-mannered, always treating me with respect. We shared breakfast each morning, our conversations polite and cordial, though rarely delving into anything personal. After breakfast, Colin would disappear for the day, busy with work that seemed to take him far from the manor. He returned just before dinner, and we would chat briefly before retiring to our separate rooms.

The servants had noticed his frequent absences, whispering among themselves that perhaps he was throwing himself into work to avoid the awkwardness of our new arrangement. I couldn't disagree. Colin had always been dedicated to his responsibilities, but now it seemed as though he was using them as a convenient escape. I couldn't blame him—after all, our marriage was not born of love or desire, but of necessity and obligation.

But there was one pressing problem that gnawed at me with each passing day. The plan I had set in motion, the lie I had spun so carefully, was beginning to unravel in the most dangerous way possible. I had claimed to be pregnant, and by the end of this week, I would be five weeks along—according to the timeline I had established. But in reality, Colin and I had yet to share even a single night together.

I had never imagined that consummating our marriage would be this difficult. Colin, for all his kindness and decency, seemed to have no interest in me beyond the surface level. He had not touched me, not once since the wedding, and I found myself in a precarious position. How could I maintain the ruse of pregnancy if we hadn't even been intimate?

The thought of failure made my stomach twist with anxiety. I had come too far, risked too much, to let it all fall apart now. I needed to act, and I needed to do it tonight.

As I stood in front of the mirror in my room, I glanced at the evening gown I had purchased before the wedding. It was a rich shade of burgundy, elegant and seductive, with a neckline that dipped just low enough to hint at the curves beneath. The fabric clung to my figure in all the right places, and as I ran my hands over the smooth silk, I felt a surge of determination.

Tonight, I would make sure that Colin and I had our first night together. There was no other option. I had to create the reality I had fabricated, and that meant taking control of the situation.

The hours seemed to crawl by as I waited for Colin to return. I busied myself with the tasks of a new mistress , familiarizing myself with the running of Ashford Manor, speaking with the servants, and ensuring that everything was in order. But my mind was elsewhere, constantly returning to the plan I had laid out in my mind.

Finally, as the sun dipped below the horizon and the evening shadows lengthened, I heard the distant sound of the front door opening. My heart raced as I made my way to the drawing room, where I knew Colin would soon join me for our customary pre-dinner conversation.

When he entered the room, I could see the faint surprise in his eyes as he took in my appearance. The gown had the desired effect, drawing his gaze and holding it for a moment longer than usual. But just as quickly, he composed himself, offering me a polite smile as he crossed the room to join me.

"Anne," he greeted, his voice as calm and measured as ever. "You look... lovely tonight."

"Thank you," I replied, allowing a hint of warmth to enter my voice. "I thought I would wear something special this evening."

Colin nodded, though his expression remained guarded. We exchanged the usual pleasantries, discussing the events of the day and the various responsibilities that had occupied our time. But beneath the surface, I could sense the tension between us, the unspoken awareness of what tonight might bring.

As we finished our conversation and the clock chimed the hour, I stood, smoothing my gown with deliberate care. "Colin," I began, my voice soft but firm, "would you join me in my room tonight?"

For a brief moment, I saw the flicker of uncertainty in his eyes, as if he wasn't sure how to respond. But then he nodded, his expression inscrutable as he rose to his feet. "Of course, Anne," he said quietly.

I led the way to my room, my heart pounding with anticipation and nerves. The door closed behind us with a soft click, sealing us in the intimate space that now felt charged with possibility.

Colin stood by the bed, his posture tense, as if unsure of how to proceed. I took a step closer, reaching out to place my hand on his chest, feeling the steady beat of his heart beneath my palm.

"We need to do this, Colin," I whispered, my voice trembling slightly. "For both of us."

He looked down at me, his eyes dark and unreadable. For a moment, I thought he might refuse, might turn and walk out of the room, leaving me to face the consequences of my deceit alone. But then he lifted his hand to cup my cheek, his touch surprisingly gentle.

"Yes, we do," he agreed, his voice low and resigned.

And with that, the distance between us began to close, our fates entwined in a way that could no longer be undone. As Colin leaned in to kiss me, I closed my eyes, willing myself to believe that this was the start of something real, something that could make the lies I had told worth it.

His touch gentle but hesitant, as if he was testing the waters of this new, fragile bond between us. I closed my eyes, letting myself melt into the moment, willing it to be the beginning of something real, something that could anchor our marriage in something more than duty and deception.

But as his lips brushed against mine, the kiss remained just that—gentle, tender, but ultimately unfulfilled. Colin pulled back slightly, his hand still resting on my cheek, and I could see the conflict in his eyes. He wanted to be there, to be close to me, but something held him back.

"Anne," he murmured, his voice laced with a mix of concern and hesitation, "I... I want to be with you, but I'm worried. You're in the early stages of pregnancy, and I don't want to do anything that could harm the baby."

His words were like a splash of cold water on my skin. I had been so focused on my plan, on the need to consummate our marriage to keep up the pretense of pregnancy, that I hadn't considered this possibility. Colin's sense of responsibility, his desire to protect what he believed was our child, was stopping him from taking that final step.

For a moment, disappointment threatened to overwhelm me. This was my chance, the moment I had been waiting for, and now it was slipping away. But I couldn't let him see that. I couldn't afford to seem indifferent to the well-being of the baby I was supposedly carrying. So I swallowed my frustration and forced a smile, nodding in agreement.

"Of course, Colin," I replied softly, trying to hide the sting of rejection. "I understand. The baby's health comes first."

He looked relieved at my response, as if a weight had been lifted from his shoulders. "Thank you, Anne," he said, brushing a strand of hair away from my face. "I just want to be careful. We'll have plenty of time for... everything else."

I nodded again, even as my mind raced to reassess the situation. I needed to get pregnant, and soon, but I couldn't push Colin without arousing suspicion. Instead, I needed to be patient, to play the long game and use the time I had wisely.

"I'd like to spend every night with you, though," I said, carefully measuring my words. "Even if we can't be... fully together yet, I'd feel better knowing we're close."

Colin seemed surprised by my request, but after a moment, he nodded in agreement. "All right, Anne," he said, his voice gentle. "We can do that."

It was a dangerous decision, one that could easily backfire. With Colin around every night, he might notice that my stomach wasn't changing, that there was no sign of the pregnancy I claimed to be experiencing. But I couldn't afford to waste the opportunity to seduce him, to create the circumstances that would make my lie a reality.

The days that followed were a delicate dance, one that required every ounce of cunning and patience I possessed. Each night, I invited Colin into my room, creating an atmosphere of intimacy without crossing the line he had drawn. We would talk, sharing the mundane details of our days, and I would inch closer to him, letting our touches linger just a little longer, our kisses grow just a little deeper.

I made sure to wear nightgowns that were both elegant and subtly alluring, hinting at what lay beneath without being overt. I could see the effect it had on Colin, the way his gaze would linger on me, the way his breath would catch when I touched him. But each time, he would pull back, reminding himself—and me—of the need to be careful for the baby's sake.

It was a slow, maddening process, one that tested my resolve and patience. But I knew that I couldn't rush him, couldn't push too hard, or I risked everything falling apart. Instead, I had to be strategic, to read his moods and gauge when the moment was right.

And when I felt the situation growing too dangerous, when I sensed that he might start to question the lack of changes in my body, I would retreat to my own room, citing fatigue or the need for rest. It was a delicate balance, but one I was determined to maintain.

This was my life now—a game of patience and deception, with everything hanging in the balance. But I had come too far to back down, too far to let my plans unravel. I would get what I wanted, even if it meant waiting just a little longer, even if it meant playing this game for as long as it took.

And when the time was right, I would make sure that my lie became the truth.

23

The Night of Seduction

The nights dragged on, each one a new opportunity, a new attempt to bridge the distance between us. I had resolved to seduce Colin, to make my fabricated pregnancy a reality, but each night ended in quiet defeat. No matter how much I tried to draw him closer, to ignite the spark that would lead us to consummate our marriage, Colin always held back.

Everynight, draping myself in the most elegant and alluring nightgowns I could find, letting the soft candlelight cast shadows that hinted at what lay beneath the silk and lace. We would sit together, talking about our day or reminiscing about the past, and I would lean into him, letting our hands brush, letting our touches linger. But when the moment came, when I thought he might finally give in, Colin would always pull away, his sense of duty to the unborn child he believed in stronger than any desire he might have felt.

It was maddening. I could see the struggle in his eyes, the way he would clench his jaw, as if physically restraining himself from crossing the line. And yet, for all his restraint, he was unfailingly kind, attentive, even sweet in a way that began to unsettle me.

At first, I had been determined, telling myself that if I couldn't seduce him, I would simply fake a miscarriage. It seemed like the most logical solution— if the lie couldn't be sustained, then I would end it before it could destroy me. But as the days turned into weeks, and Colin's gentle treatment of me continued, I found myself wavering.

Colin was nothing like the cold, distant husband I had feared he would be. Instead, he was considerate, always making sure I was comfortable, that I was taken care of. Every morning, he would ask how I was feeling, if I needed anything. At breakfast, he would pour my tea, his touch light on my hand as he set the cup in front of me. In the evenings, when we would sit together in my room, he would often reach out to rub my belly, his touch so tender it nearly brought tears to my eyes.

"You know," he said softly, his voice full of a quiet wonder that made my heart ache, "I can't stop thinking about the future. When the baby is born, they'll be so close in age to Adelaide's child. They'll grow up together, like siblings. It's... it's something I've started looking forward to more than I ever expected."

His words were like a dagger to my heart. I had known Colin would take his responsibilities seriously, but I hadn't anticipated just how much he would invest in this imagined future. He was already planning for the child's life, already picturing the joy it would bring, not just to us, but to Adelaide and her baby as well. The sincerity in his voice, the warmth in his eyes as he spoke about our future, made the lie I was living all the more unbearable.

I had been prepared to deceive him, to manipulate him into bed, and if that failed, to fabricate a miscarriage and move on. But now, with each passing day, the idea of doing that to him became more unbearable. How could I destroy the hope in his eyes, the excitement he had for this child that didn't even exist yet? How could I be the one to shatter the future he was already planning for, the bond he was already forming with a child he believed was growing inside me?

But I was running out of time. The weeks were slipping by, and soon, my supposed pregnancy would be impossible to maintain without physical evidence. My stomach, which should have been showing signs of growth, remained stubbornly flat, a constant reminder that I was living on borrowed time.

Each night, I would try again, mustering the courage to push a little further, to cross the line that Colin had drawn. I would let my fingers trail over his chest, lean in closer when we kissed, trying to stir something in him that would break his resolve. But he always pulled back, his hand moving to my stomach as if reminding himself of the life he believed he was protecting.

And with every failed attempt, my frustration grew. But it wasn't just frustration at the situation—it was frustration at myself, at the growing confusion that tangled my thoughts and emotions. Colin's kindness, his gentle care, had begun to chip away at the wall I had built around my heart. The man who had once been nothing more than a means to an end was becoming someone I didn't want to hurt, someone I didn't want to deceive.

But what choice did I have?

The thought of faking a miscarriage had once seemed like an easy out, a way to free myself from the lies without too much fallout. But now, the idea of watching Colin's face crumble with the news, of seeing the hope die in his eyes, was more than I could bear. He was already planning for a future with this child, dreaming of a life that I had fabricated, and the thought of taking that away from him filled me with a deep, aching guilt.

But the longer I waited, the more dangerous my situation became. The more I hesitated, the more impossible it would be to maintain the lie. I was running out of time, and I knew it. But with each passing day, the decision only grew harder. I couldn't back down now. I had come too far, and the time to make this lie a reality was running out. I needed to act, and I needed to do it tonight.

As Colin stood to leave, offering me the same chaste goodnight kiss as always, I found myself unable to let the moment end. The pressure of time and my growing guilt weighed heavily on me, pushing me to take a bold step.

I followed him out of the room, my heart pounding in my chest. I found him in the drawing room, pouring himself a glass of wine. The rich scent of the alcohol filled the air, and I watched as he took a long, slow sip, his shoulders visibly relaxing as the tension of the day melted away.

For a moment, I simply stood there, watching him. There was something about the sight of Colin unwinding, his guard lowered, that made me hesitate. But I couldn't afford to stop now. I needed to make this work.

"Colin," I said softly, stepping into the room. He looked up, surprised to see me, but his expression quickly shifted to concern.

"Anne," he said, setting down his glass as he moved toward me. "You shouldn't be drinking. It's not good for the baby."

I forced a smile, hoping it looked playful rather than strained. "I know," I replied, glancing at the glass in his hand. "But I was hoping you might share just a little with me. I can't have any wine because of the baby, but maybe... if you kissed me, I could taste it that way."

Colin blinked, clearly taken aback by my suggestion. For a moment, I thought he might refuse, might pull away as he had so many times before. But then, his gaze softened, and he chuckled, a sound that was both surprised and amused.

"Anne," he said, shaking his head slightly, "you really are something."

I took a step closer, closing the distance between us. "Please," I whispered, my voice barely audible. "Just a taste."

He hesitated, his eyes searching mine for any sign of doubt. But there was none. I had made my choice, and I needed him to make his. Finally, he nodded, lifting the glass to his lips once more before leaning in to kiss me.

The taste of the wine was sweet on his lips, a heady blend of flavors that sent a shiver down my spine. But it wasn't just the wine—it was the way he kissed me, with a passion that had been so carefully restrained until now. I could feel the tension in him melting away, replaced by something warmer, more urgent.

As the kiss deepened, I felt a surge of determination. This was my chance, my last opportunity to turn this marriage into what it needed to be. I reached up, letting my fingers trail down the buttons of his waistcoat, loosening them as I pressed closer to him.

Colin didn't stop me. Instead, he wrapped his arms around me, pulling me against him with a need that mirrored my own. I could feel the warmth of his body through the thin fabric of my nightgown, and it gave me the courage to push further.

Slowly, I began to reveal more of myself, letting the straps of my gown slip from my shoulders, exposing the soft curve of my cleavage and the smooth line of my thighs. Colin's breath hitched as his gaze followed the movement, his eyes darkening with desire.

I took his hand, guiding it to the bare skin of my thigh, letting him feel the warmth of my body, the softness of my flesh. "Colin," I murmured, my voice husky with anticipation, "I want you. Please..."

He groaned softly, a sound that sent a thrill of victory through me. I had him. Finally, I had him.

With a sudden movement, Colin grabbed me, lifting me onto the table behind us. The cool wood against my skin was a stark contrast to the heat of his touch, and I gasped as he kissed me again, this time with a hunger that left no room for hesitation.

His lips were soft yet demanding, and I responded eagerly, my arms wrapping around his neck as he pulled me closer. His hands squeezed my thighs, and I could feel the heat radiating from his body. I knew that we shouldn't be doing this, not here in the middle of the night, but I couldn't bring myself to care.

"What about our baby, Anne?" he asked hesitantly, pulling away slightly. I looked into his eyes, seeing the concern etched on his face. We had only had sex once after we got married, and I knew that he was worried about the consequences.

"Our baby will be fine," I reassured him, kissing his neck. "I want this, Colin. I want you." He hesitated for a moment, but then he nodded, and I could feel the tension in his body ease.

Without wasting any more time, I moved my hand to his crotch and squeezed. Colin's cock was already engorged and hard, and I kept squeezing, making him moaned. "Do it right away," I demanded, and Colin undid his pants.

Colin didn't need any more encouragement. He undid his pants, and his cock sprang free, hard and ready. I lifted my nightgown, revealing my bare breasts and wet pussy. Colin didn't waste any time. He slid his cock inside me, filling me up in a way that made me gasp. We did it with me sitting on the table and Colin standing. Colin's hands gripped my hips, holding me in place as he began to thrust. I wrapped my legs around his waist, pulling him deeper inside me. Our bodies moved together in a rhythm that was both familiar and exciting.

"Yes, Colin, yes," I moaned, my nails digging into his back. "Harder, fuck me harder."

Colin responded by increasing his pace, his cock sliding in and out of me with a slickness that made me wetter than I'd ever been before. I could feel myself getting close to orgasm, and I knew Colin was too.

"Anne, you feel so good," he whispered in my ear, and I couldn't agree more. We continued to fuck, lost in our own world, until we both reached our peak. Our moans filled the room, and I couldn't help but scream out his name. "Colin, yes, yes, right there!" I cried out, feeling his cock hit all the right spots.

"I'm going to cum," he gasped, his thrusts becoming erratic.

"Cum inside me," I commanded, wanting to feel his warmth fill me up.

Colin groaned in pleasure, holding onto me tightly as he came inside me. I could feel his cock twitching inside me as he released his load. I squeezed him tighter, milking every last drop. I followed soon after, my orgasm rippling through my body like a wave.

We stayed like that for a moment, our bodies still connected, our breathing heavy. Colin pulled out of me and kissed me gently.

24

The Morning Light

When I woke up, the first thing I noticed was the warmth of another body nestled against mine. I blinked, my mind slowly coming to terms with the reality of Anne curled up beside me on the drawing room sofa. Her breathing was steady, her face peaceful in sleep, but the memories of last night began to trickle back, and with them came a wave of guilt and confusion.

I sighed heavily, running a hand through my hair, trying to piece together the events of the night. I remembered her soft whispers, the way she had kissed me, asking for just a taste of the wine I was drinking because she couldn't have any due to the baby. I had given in, let my guard down, and now, with the morning light streaming through the windows, the weight of that decision pressed down on me.

I looked down at Anne, still peacefully asleep, and the guilt only deepened. How could I have been so reckless? She was carrying our child, and I should have been more careful, more mindful of her condition. The responsibility of protecting her and the baby was mine, and I had failed.

As I began to carefully disentangle myself from her embrace, Anne stirred, her eyes fluttering open. She blinked a few times, her gaze finding mine as she slowly came to full awareness.

"Good morning," she murmured, her voice still thick with sleep.

"Good morning," I replied softly, forcing a smile that I didn't entirely feel.

Anne stretched slightly, sitting up and adjusting the blanket around her. "I didn't expect to wake up here," she said with a small, shy smile. "But I suppose last night was... different."

I nodded, my thoughts still clouded with the remnants of guilt. "Anne, about last night... I don't think it was wise, given your condition. You're in the early stages of pregnancy, and I should have been more careful. We should have been more careful."

Her smile faltered slightly, but she quickly masked it with understanding. "Colin, the baby is fine. I'm fine. Last night meant a lot to me... it felt like we were finally connecting as husband and wife."

Her words tugged at something deep within me, a mix of relief and unease. I wanted to be the husband she needed, the father our child deserved, but I couldn't shake the feeling that I had crossed a line.

"Still," I said, my tone more serious, "I think it would be best if we kept our distance, at least for now. I don't want to do anything that could put the baby at risk."

Anne looked at me, her eyes searching mine, and after a moment, she nodded slowly. "If that's what you think is best, Colin, I'll respect that." She hesitated, then added, "But... I don't want to be alone every night. Can we at least... share the same bed, even if we're not... you know?"

I hesitated, torn between my desire to comfort her and my fear of repeating my mistake. But the thought of leaving her alone, especially after the way she had opened up to me, felt wrong. So I nodded, offering her a small, reassuring smile. "We can share the same bed. We'll take things slowly."

Anne's expression softened, and she reached out to gently squeeze my hand. "Thank you, Colin. That's all I need."

We sat there for a few moments in a comfortable silence, the weight of the night's events still hanging between us, but with a sense of understanding that hadn't been there before. It was as though we were both coming to terms with the reality of our marriage, the responsibilities that came with it, and the need to move forward together, however uncertain the path might be.

Finally, Anne let out a soft sigh and stood up, smoothing her dress as she prepared to leave the room. "I should get ready for the day," she said, her tone light, though there was a lingering seriousness in her eyes. "Will you join me for breakfast?"

"I'll join you," I replied, my voice still carrying the weight of everything unsaid. "But I need to take care of a few things first."

She nodded, her expression guarded but understanding. "I'll see you at breakfast, then."

As she left the room, I couldn't shake the sense of unease that settled over me. The connection we had shared last night had been real, but it had also felt like a mistake—a mistake that I couldn't afford to make again. I had to protect her, protect the baby, and that meant being more cautious, more disciplined.

I stood up and made my way to the sideboard where the decanter of wine still sat, remnants of last night's temptation. I reached for it, but hesitated, the memory of Anne's playful request for a taste echoing in my mind.

"Colin," she had said, her eyes gleaming with mischief, "if I can't drink because of the baby, maybe you could kiss me instead."

I shook my head hard. "You're out of your mind, Colin! She's pregnant and carrying your child!"

I tried to erase all thoughts of last night and walked out of the drawing room. I didn't want to linger here and make myself remember the events of last night because despite the guilt that arose, I felt pleasure and I wanted it again.

As I quietly left the drawing room and made my way to my own chambers, I couldn't shake the feeling that I had crossed a line, one that I couldn't uncross. The connection I had felt with Anne last night was real, but it had been born of weakness, of a momentary lapse in judgment. And now, I had to face the consequences.

I splashed cold water on my face, trying to wash away the remnants of the night before, but the weight in my chest remained. I had to protect Anne, to ensure that she and the baby were safe. That meant keeping my distance, even if it meant sacrificing the fragile bond we had begun to form.

But as I dressed and prepared for the day ahead, I couldn't help but wonder if I was doing the right thing. Was distance really the answer, or was I only pushing her away when she needed me most? The thought nagged at me, but

I pushed it aside, focusing on what I believed was my duty.

For the sake of our child, I had to be strong. I had to put aside my own desires, my own needs, and focus on what was best for Anne and the baby. Even if it meant keeping my distance, even if it meant denying the connection that had sparked between us.

As I left my chambers and headed downstairs, I resolved to be more careful, more disciplined. Last night had been a mistake, a lapse that I couldn't afford to repeat. For the sake of our child, I had to be better. I had to be the husband Anne needed, even if it meant keeping my heart at a distance.

But as I stepped into the quiet morning light, I couldn't shake the feeling that something had changed between us—something that couldn't be undone, no matter how hard I tried.

25

The Unexpected Ache

The events of that night had been unexpected, a mix of victory and confusion that left me reeling. When I had first set out to seduce Colin, to draw him into the web of my carefully constructed lies, I had never truly believed that it would work. But it had—at least for one night. I had succeeded in making him mine, in consummating the marriage that had started with so many deceptions. Yet, as the days passed, the satisfaction of that success began to fade, replaced by a gnawing uncertainty.

Pregnancy wasn't guaranteed by a single night together, and I knew I had to continue my efforts. I had to make sure that what I had claimed would become real. So, night after night, I found myself repeating the same delicate dance, trying to reignite the connection we had shared. I wore the same alluring gowns, whispered the same sweet words, and leaned in just a little closer, hoping that he would respond as he had before.

But something had changed. Colin began to pull away, his once-warm smiles becoming more distant, his touch more hesitant. At first, I thought it was my imagination, a trick of my own insecurity playing on my mind. But as the days turned into weeks, the distance between us grew more palpable, a chasm that I couldn't seem to bridge.

I couldn't understand it. Why was he pulling away? Did he suspect something? Had he begun to realize that our marriage was nothing more than a trap, that he was merely a victim in my carefully laid plans? Or was it something else entirely, something deeper that I couldn't see?

The uncertainty gnawed at me, fraying the edges of my carefully constructed composure. I told myself that it didn't matter, that this marriage wasn't supposed to be about love or even mutual benefit. It was simply a means to an end, a way to secure my future and escape the looming threats that had once surrounded me. Colin was supposed to be nothing more than a pawn, a man caught in a game he didn't know he was playing.

But the more he pulled away, the more I found myself questioning everything.

One night, after yet another failed attempt to draw him close, I finally broke. I had planned everything so perfectly, set every detail in motion, but now it was all unraveling, and I didn't know how to stop it.

We had been sitting in the drawing room, the fire crackling softly in the hearth. I had moved closer to him, brushing my fingers against his arm as I spoke, letting my voice drop to a whisper, trying to reignite the spark that had once been there. But instead of responding, Colin gently pulled away, his expression pained.

"Anne," he said softly, "I think we need to stop this."

His words were like a blow to the chest, knocking the breath out of me. "Stop what?" I asked, my voice trembling despite my best efforts to keep it steady.

"This... trying to force something that isn't there," he replied, his gaze dropping to the floor. "I don't want to hurt you, but I'm just... I'm not sure this is right."

His rejection stung more than I could have imagined. It wasn't supposed to hurt like this. I wasn't supposed to care. This marriage was a trap, I reminded myself, a means to an end, not a love story. But the pain was real, sharp and deep, and it took all my strength not to break down in front of him.

"I understand," I whispered, the words barely audible. I forced a smile, hoping he wouldn't see the tears welling up in my eyes. "You're right. Maybe we've been trying too hard."

Colin nodded, relief washing over his features as he mistook my response for agreement. "Thank you, Anne," he said, his voice softening. "I just... I want to do what's best for both of us."

I nodded, unable to trust my voice to say anything more. When he stood to leave, I remained where I was, staring into the flickering flames of the fire, the tears now freely streaming down my cheeks.

Once he was gone, I couldn't hold back the sobs that had been building in my chest. I cried, harder than I had in years, the weight of everything crashing down on me at once. I didn't understand it—why was I hurting like this? Why did his rejection feel like a knife twisting in my heart?

This marriage was never supposed to be about love. It was a trap, with me as the hunter and Colin as the prey. I had orchestrated everything, planned every detail, and yet now, I found myself caught in my own web, the lines between truth and deception blurring in ways I hadn't anticipated.

The tears wouldn't stop, and I curled up on the sofa, hugging my knees to my chest as the reality of my situation pressed down on me. I was supposed to be in control, supposed to be the one pulling the strings. But now, it felt like everything was slipping through my fingers, like I was losing something I hadn't even realized I wanted.

What was happening to me? Why did I care so much about what Colin thought, about how he felt? This was just a marriage of convenience, a way to secure my future. And yet, the thought of him pulling away, of him rejecting me, filled me with a pain I couldn't explain.

Was it possible that somewhere along the way, I had started to care for him? Was it possible that I had begun to fall for the man I had trapped? The thought terrified me, because if that were true, then everything I had built was at risk of crumbling around me.

But in that moment, as I cried into the empty room, I couldn't find the strength to deny it.

26

The Weight of Regret

I had convinced myself that asking Anne to stop flirting with me was the right thing to do. I was just a man—an ordinary man who couldn't keep his resolve intact when she looked at me like that, when she touched me with such tenderness. I had already lost control once, on that night when we'd given in to our desires, and I regretted it deeply. How could I have been so reckless? Anne was four weeks pregnant—how could I have let things go so far?

But as the morning light streamed into the manor, a strange emptiness settled over me when Anne didn't join me for breakfast. Her absence left the dining room feeling cold and lifeless, and the food on my plate felt like ash in my mouth. I tried to focus on my meal, but I couldn't shake the uneasy feeling that something was wrong.

Unable to ignore it any longer, I called for Harris, the butler, to inquire about Anne's whereabouts.

"Harris," I began, trying to keep my voice steady, "where is Lady Ashford? Why isn't she at breakfast?"

Harris hesitated, his expression carefully neutral. "Lady Ashford mentioned that she had no appetite this morning, my lord. She requested to take her meal in her room, but later informed the staff that she didn't wish to eat at all."

A pang of guilt hit me square in the chest. Anne, with no appetite? That wasn't like her. Could it be because of what I had said last night? I had heard her crying after I left the drawing room, but I had told myself it was better to leave her alone, to give her the space she needed. Now, I wasn't so sure.

Feeling increasingly unsettled, I dismissed Harris and called for Mrs. Whitmore, the head maid. She was a woman of experience and had seen many pregnancies during her years of service. If anyone could give me insight, it would be her.

"Mrs. Whitmore," I asked as she entered the room, "do you know if Lady Ashford's loss of appetite is due to her pregnancy? She's been... different lately, and I'm concerned."

Mrs. Whitmore studied me with a keen, understanding eye before she answered, her tone gentle yet firm. "My lord, it's quite common for pregnant women to experience difficulty with their appetite, especially in the early stages. Mornings can be particularly tough on them. Certain foods or even smells may become intolerable. It's not just physical, though—pregnancy can bring about heightened emotions as well. They may find themselves more sensitive, both physically and emotionally, and they often seek comfort and reassurance from their husbands during this vulnerable time."

Her words hung in the air, and I felt a wave of panic rising in my chest. Had I been so blind? Was this why Anne had been acting differently toward me lately? Was it because of the baby, because she needed me, and I had pushed her away?

"Mrs. Whitmore," I asked carefully, "do you think... do you think she's been trying to be closer to me because of the baby?"

Mrs. Whitmore nodded, her expression softening with a touch of empathy. "It's very possible, my lord. Sometimes, a pregnant woman feels an instinctive need to be near her husband, to feel supported and loved. The changes they go through can be overwhelming, and they often find solace in their partner's presence. It's a natural reaction."

Her explanation sent another pang of guilt through me. I had been so focused on doing what I thought was right, on keeping my distance to protect her and the baby, that I hadn't realized the effect it was having on her. I had left her feeling isolated, when all she wanted was to be close to me, to be reassured during this uncertain time.

I ran a hand through my hair in frustration, trying to make sense of everything. How could I have been so blind? How could I have missed the signs?

I stood abruptly, the chair scraping against the floor as I pushed it back. "Thank you, Mrs. Whitmore. I need to see Anne."

She nodded and gave a small, encouraging smile. "I'm sure Lady Ashford would appreciate that, my lord. Sometimes, all they need is to know that you're there for them."

As I made my way to Anne's room, my mind raced with thoughts of how to fix this, how to bridge the gap I had unwittingly created. I had been so concerned with not repeating my mistake that I had failed to see what Anne truly needed from me. I couldn't let that continue. I had to make this right, to show her that I was here for her, that I wouldn't let her go through this alone.

When I reached her door, I hesitated for a moment, taking a deep breath to steady myself. Then I knocked softly and waited.

"Anne? It's me, Colin. May I come in?"

There was a pause, and then I heard her soft voice from the other side. "Come in."

I pushed the door open and stepped inside, my heart heavy with the weight of my earlier actions. Anne was sitting by the window, her hands folded in her lap, her eyes red-rimmed from crying. The sight of her like that nearly broke me.

"Anne," I began, my voice cracking slightly, "I'm sorry. I've been an idiot. I thought I was doing the right thing by keeping my distance, but I see now that I was wrong. I never meant to make you feel alone."

She looked up at me, her eyes searching mine for sincerity. "I just... I just wanted to feel close to you, Colin," she said, her voice trembling. "But every time I tried, it felt like you were pulling away. I know this marriage wasn't what either of us planned, but... we're in this together now, and I need you."

Her words hit me like a punch to the gut, and I crossed the room in a few quick strides, kneeling beside her chair. "You're right," I admitted, taking her hands in mine. "We are in this together, and I'm sorry I made you feel otherwise. I've been so focused on protecting you and the baby that I didn't realize I was hurting you in the process. But that ends now. I'm here, Anne. I'm with you, and I'm not going anywhere."

She looked at me for a long moment, her eyes filled with a mix of relief and lingering doubt. "You mean that?"

"I do," I said firmly, squeezing her hands. "We're going to get through this together, and I promise I won't let you feel alone again."

A small smile tugged at the corners of her mouth, and she nodded, a tear slipping down her cheek. I reached up to gently wipe it away, my heart aching at the sight of her vulnerability.

"I'm sorry, too," she whispered. "For everything."

"Let's not worry about the past," I said softly. "Let's focus on what's ahead."

And as I held her close, I knew that I had to make good on that promise, for both our sakes. The path ahead might be uncertain, but it was one we would walk together, no matter what.

27

The Weight of a Lie

After the incident in my room, things between Colin and me took an unexpected turn for the better. Colin seemed to realize how isolated I had felt, and he began making a conscious effort to be there for me. Every morning, we had breakfast together, sharing quiet moments over tea and toast. He even started coming home early, ensuring we spent time together before dinner. At night, he would sit with me, his hand gently resting on my belly, and we'd talk for hours—about the day, about the future, and sometimes about things that made me feel vulnerable in ways I hadn't anticipated.

It should have been everything I wanted—everything I had worked so hard to achieve. And yet, the more time we spent together, the more uneasy I became.

One evening, after a particularly long day, Colin and I sat by the fire in the drawing room. His hand, as it often did now, rested on my belly, his thumb tracing slow, soothing circles over my skin. I leaned into him, trying to ignore the pang of guilt that came with every gentle touch.

"When do you think your belly will start to show?" he asked softly, his voice filled with anticipation. "I can't wait to see it grow, like Adelaide's."

I swallowed hard, forcing a smile as I placed my hand over his. "It will take a few more weeks," I said, my voice steady despite the turmoil inside me. "Adelaide is more than seven months along, after all."

Colin nodded, his gaze focused on my stomach as if willing it to start growing right then and there. "I know," he murmured, a smile tugging at the corners of his mouth. "But I'm just so excited. I can't wait to meet our baby, to hold them in my arms."

His words struck me deeply, the warmth in his voice contrasting sharply with the cold dread that had settled in my chest. I knew my belly wouldn't start to grow anytime soon—not unless I could make this lie a reality. The pressure was mounting, but I couldn't let him see that.

"Colin," I whispered, leaning in closer and pressing a kiss to his jawline, "we'll get there. Just be patient with me."

He turned his head slightly, capturing my lips in a tender kiss. "I'm always patient with you, Anne," he murmured against my lips. "But I can't help being excited. I've never felt this way before."

I deepened the kiss, hoping to distract him from the conversation that was growing too dangerous. My hands found their way to the buttons of his shirt, undoing them slowly, deliberately, as if each movement could erase the doubts in my mind.

"Maybe we should focus on enjoying the present," I suggested, my voice soft and inviting. "We have all the time in the world to worry about the future."

Colin chuckled, the sound low and warm, as he pulled me closer. "I like the way you think," he said, his voice tinged with amusement. "You always know how to make me forget about everything else."

We kissed again, this time with more urgency, more need. I wanted to lose myself in the moment, to forget about the lie I was living and the weight of the deception that threatened to crush me. For a while, it worked. Colin's touch was gentle, his kisses filled with a tenderness that made my heart ache. He treated me with such care, as if I were fragile, breakable, and it only made the guilt more unbearable.

When we finally pulled apart, breathless and flushed, Colin rested his forehead against mine. "You're amazing, you know that?" he whispered, his voice filled with sincerity.

I smiled, though it felt bittersweet. "And you're everything I need," I replied, my words laced with the truth of how much I had come to rely on him, even if he didn't know the full extent of it.

Later that night, as we lay in bed together, I found myself staring at the ceiling, unable to sleep. Colin was beside me, his arm draped over my waist, his breathing slow and steady as he slept. I should have felt content, secure in the knowledge that my plan was working. We had made love again, as we had many times before, and with each time, I felt a little closer to turning my lie into the truth.

But instead of relief, I felt a growing sense of unease. The more time I spent with Colin, the harder it became to maintain the facade. He was so attentive, so kind, and it was becoming increasingly difficult to reconcile that with the lies I had told. Every time he touched my belly, every time he whispered sweet words about our future, it felt like a knife twisting in my heart.

One evening, a few days later, as we sat in the drawing room again, Colin's voice broke through my thoughts. "Anne," he began, his tone hesitant, "I've been thinking... Have you thought about names for the baby?"

His question caught me off guard, and I looked up at him, startled. "Names?" I echoed, trying to buy myself a moment to think. "I... I haven't given it much thought yet."

Colin smiled, his hand moving to cup my cheek. "I know it's early, but I can't help wondering. I was thinking... if it's a boy, maybe we could name him after my father. And if it's a girl... well, I'll let you choose. Something beautiful, like you."

I forced a laugh, though it sounded hollow even to my own ears. "That sounds lovely, Colin," I said, leaning into his touch. "We'll have plenty of time to decide."

He kissed me again, and I felt the familiar warmth of his embrace, the way his presence seemed to calm my racing thoughts. But even as I returned his kiss, a bitter taste lingered in my mouth. How long could I keep this up? How long before he started to notice that my belly wasn't growing, that the lies I had spun were beginning to unravel?

"Let's not worry about names just yet," I whispered against his lips, my fingers tangling in his hair. "Let's focus on us, right now."

Colin smiled, nodding as he pulled me closer. "You're right," he agreed, his voice low and filled with affection. "We have plenty of time."

We kissed again, slowly, deeply, as if we could lose ourselves in each other and forget about the world outside. But even as I melted into his arms, the weight of the lie I was living pressed down on me, heavier with each passing day.

As we lay in bed that night, his arms wrapped around me, I stared into the darkness, my mind racing with thoughts of the future. I had gotten everything I wanted—Colin was mine, and our marriage was solidified by the physical bond we shared. But instead of feeling victorious, I felt trapped in the very web I had spun.

I knew that time was running out. Sooner or later, Colin would start to ask more questions, and I wouldn't be able to distract him forever. I had to get pregnant, and soon, or everything I had worked for would come crashing down around me.

But as I listened to Colin's steady breathing beside me, his arm draped protectively over my waist, I couldn't shake the feeling that I was on borrowed time. The truth was like a storm on the horizon, threatening to destroy everything in its path.

For now, Colin remained blissfully unaware, lost in the dreams of a future that might never come to pass. And I... I was left to grapple with the weight of my choices, knowing that each day brought me closer to the moment when the truth would be impossible to hide.

28

The Shattered Illusion

As the days turned into weeks, my married life with Colin began to take on a warmth I hadn't expected. We had settled into a routine—shared breakfasts, evenings spent together by the fire, and nights filled with tender intimacy. Colin was everything I had ever hoped for in a husband, kind and attentive, with a gentle touch that spoke of his growing affection for me. But beneath the surface, a gnawing guilt festered, a constant reminder of the deception that had brought us to this point.

Each time Colin placed his hand on my belly, each time he spoke with eager anticipation about our future child, the weight of my lies bore down on me with increasing intensity. I couldn't help but reflect on the lengths I had gone to in order to secure this marriage—the drugs, the manipulation, the fabricated pregnancy. I had trapped him in a web of deceit, and now that web was beginning to unravel.

But something unexpected had happened along the way. Somewhere in the midst of all the scheming and pretending, my feelings for Colin had begun to change. What had started as a means to an end had slowly transformed into something deeper, something real. I found myself drawn to him, not just as a husband I needed to keep close, but as a man I genuinely cared for. And that scared me more than anything.

I couldn't lose Colin now. I didn't know when it had happened—when my feelings had started to deepen—but I knew that they had. Every day, as we spent more time together, as we grew closer, my affection for him grew stronger. Our marriage may have been born out of lies, but it had blossomed into something that felt achingly real, at least on my end.

But with that deepening affection came a growing sense of dread. The chasm between us, created by my lies, seemed impossibly wide, and I knew that one day it would have to be crossed. I would have to tell him the truth—about the baby that didn't exist, about the way I had trapped him. But how could I? The thought of seeing the love in his eyes turn to hatred, of losing him forever, was more than I could bear.

I resolved to wait, to build our relationship further, to create something so strong that it could withstand the truth when I was finally ready to reveal it. But time was running out. I knew it was only a matter of weeks before Colin would start to ask questions about my pregnancy, before he would notice that my belly wasn't growing as it should.

I was so caught up in my own internal struggle, so focused on finding the right moment to be honest, that I didn't see the next storm brewing on the horizon.

It started with whispers—snide comments at social gatherings, pointed looks from women who had once greeted me with smiles. At first, I dismissed them as nothing more than the usual gossip, the idle chatter of bored aristocrats. But as the days passed, the whispers grew louder, more persistent, until they became impossible to ignore.

One afternoon, as I sat in the drawing room, a letter was delivered to me by one of the housemaids. It was from an old acquaintance, Lady Beatrice, a woman known for her sharp tongue and keen sense of the social undercurrents that flowed through London's elite. I opened the letter with a sense of unease, and as I read the words scrawled across the page, my heart sank.

The rumors were spreading like wildfire. Earl Eric, furious and humiliated by my marriage to Colin, had begun to spread vicious lies about me. He claimed that the child I was supposedly carrying wasn't Colin's at all, but his. He insinuated that I had married Colin to cover up my own indiscretions, to legitimize a child conceived in sin.

The blood drained from my face as I read the letter, my hands trembling with a mix of fear and rage. How dare he? How dare he try to ruin me, to destroy the life I had so carefully built with Colin? But beneath the anger, a deeper fear took hold. If these rumors reached Colin's ears, if he believed even for a moment that they might be true...

I couldn't let that happen. I had to find a way to stop this, to protect my marriage, to protect the fragile bond I had forged with Colin. But how? The rumors were already spreading, and I knew how quickly society's judgment could turn against a woman. My carefully constructed life was on the brink of collapse, and I felt powerless to stop it.

I needed to tell Colin the truth. I knew that. But the thought of it terrified me. How could I confess everything now, in the midst of this storm? How could I reveal the lies that had built our marriage while also trying to defend myself against these vile accusations?

Tears pricked at the corners of my eyes as I clutched the letter in my hands. I had wanted to be honest with Colin, to come clean when the time was right. But now, with these rumors swirling around us, that time had been stolen from me. I was out of options, out of time, and the walls were closing in.

I knew I couldn't delay any longer. I had to speak to Colin, had to try to salvage what little I could of our marriage before it was too late. But as I rose to my feet, the letter clutched in my hand, a sense of dread washed over me. This was it—the moment I had been dreading, the moment when everything could come crashing down.

I took a deep breath, steeling myself for what was to come. There was no turning back now. I had to face the consequences of my actions, and pray that the love we had begun to build would be enough to see us through.

As I made my way through the corridors of Ashford Manor, my heart pounded in my chest, each step heavier than the last. I couldn't shake the feeling that the universe had other surprises in store for me, surprises that would test the very foundation of our marriage. And in that moment, I wasn't sure if we were strong enough to survive them.

The letter from Lady Beatrice was crumpled in my hand, a tangible reminder of the vicious rumors that were spreading through London like wildfire. I had hoped to reach Colin before the rumors did, to explain myself and somehow salvage our fragile marriage. But as I neared his study, I could hear raised voices coming from within, and a cold dread settled over me.

Taking a deep breath, I pushed the door open, only to find Colin standing by the window, his back to me. His posture was tense, his hands clenched into fists at his sides. He was speaking in low, angry tones with Harris, the butler, who stood quietly, his head bowed.

The moment I stepped inside, Colin's voice cut off, and he turned to face me. The look in his eyes was one I had never seen before—cold, furious, and filled with a level of suspicion that made my blood run cold.

"Anne," he said, his voice taut with barely controlled anger. "I was just hearing some very interesting news. Perhaps you'd care to explain."

I swallowed hard, trying to steady my trembling hands as I closed the door behind me. "Colin, I—"

"You've heard the rumors, I assume?" he interrupted, his tone biting. "The ones that claim the child you're carrying isn't mine, but belongs to Earl Eric?"

My breath caught in my throat. So, he had already heard. The very thing I had feared had come to pass, and now there was no going back. "Colin, please," I began, my voice trembling. "It's not true. I swear to you, there's nothing between me and Earl Eric. These are just lies he's spreading to ruin us."

Colin's jaw tightened, and he took a step closer, his eyes boring into mine. "Then tell me, Anne. Tell me why these rumors started. Tell me why Earl Eric would say such a thing."

I opened my mouth to speak, but the words wouldn't come. How could I explain the tangled web of lies I had woven, the lengths I had gone to in order to trap him into marriage? How could I tell him that there was no child, that the pregnancy was a fabrication? The truth was too dangerous, too damning. And so, I hesitated, my silence only fueling his growing anger.

"You can't, can you?" Colin spat, his voice shaking with fury. "You can't even defend yourself. What am I supposed to believe, Anne? What am I supposed to think when you can't even give me a straight answer?"

"Colin, please, just listen to me—" I reached out for him, but he pulled away, his expression one of disgust and betrayal.

"I trusted you, Anne," he said, his voice cracking with emotion. "I let myself believe that this marriage could be something real, that we could build a life together. And now... now I don't know what to believe."

My heart shattered at the pain in his voice, at the distance that had suddenly opened up between us. I had wanted to be honest with him, to come clean about everything, but now it felt impossible. The more I tried to find the words, the more they slipped through my fingers, leaving me helpless in the face of his anger.

"Colin, I'm begging you," I whispered, tears welling up in my eyes. "Don't do this. Don't believe these lies. I know I've made mistakes, but I care about you, about us. I need you to believe me."

But my pleas fell on deaf ears. Colin shook his head, his eyes cold and distant. "How can I believe you, Anne? How can I believe anything you say when you can't even tell me the truth?"

The silence that followed was deafening, the chasm between us growing wider with each passing moment. I could see the hurt in his eyes, the betrayal that cut deeper than any words could express. And I knew, in that moment, that I had lost him. The love we had begun to build, the trust we had started to form, was crumbling before my eyes.

"I can't do this," Colin finally said, his voice hollow. "I can't stay here and pretend everything is fine when I don't know what to believe. I need time to think, to figure out what the truth is."

He turned away from me, his shoulders slumped with the weight of his despair. "I'm going to stay at the lodge for a few days," he said quietly. "I need space."

My heart sank, a cold dread settling in my stomach. "Colin, please—"

But he was already walking away, his steps heavy and deliberate as he left the room. The door closed behind him with a finality that sent a shiver down my spine.

I stood there, alone in the silence, the weight of my guilt pressing down on me like a suffocating blanket. I had wanted to tell him the truth, but now... now it felt like it was too late. The damage had been done, and the love I had fought so hard to protect was slipping through my fingers.

As the tears finally fell, I knew that I had made a terrible mistake. I had been so focused on securing this marriage, on trapping Colin in my web of lies, that I hadn't realized how fragile it all was. And now, it was crumbling around me, leaving me with nothing but the hollow echoes of what could have been.

All I could do was hope that, somehow, Colin would find it in his heart to forgive me. But as the cold reality set in, I feared that forgiveness was the one thing I might never receive.

29

A Crumbling Trust

As I left the room, my heart was heavy with a sadness I hadn't expected. The rumors about Anne had come as a brutal shock, one that had left me reeling. I had been looking forward to the future, to the baby growing in Anne's belly, to the life we were building together. But now, the foundation of that future felt as though it was being torn apart, brick by brick.

The thought that the child might not be mine, that Anne could have betrayed me, was something I couldn't bear to consider. But how could I ignore it? The rumors were vicious, and they had already spread like wildfire through London's elite. I knew how these things worked—rumors didn't just appear out of nowhere. They had a way of taking root in a small kernel of truth, growing into something much larger, much darker.

And the fact that Anne couldn't give me a straight answer only fueled my doubts. If the rumors were baseless, why hadn't she denied them outright? Why couldn't she look me in the eye and tell me the truth?

My mind was a whirlwind of confusion and fear as I made my way to the lodge, seeking the solitude I desperately needed to sort through my thoughts. I had wanted to believe in Anne, in the life we were building together. I had let myself grow attached to the idea of our future, of the child I thought we were bringing into the world. But now, all of that seemed to be slipping away.

I tried to make sense of it all. Earl Eric had always been a thorn in my side, a man with a reputation that preceded him. But to spread such vicious lies? It didn't add up—unless he had some reason to believe they were true.

I shook my head, trying to dispel the doubts gnawing at me. I had seen how much Anne wanted this marriage to work, how she had put on a brave face despite the challenges we had faced. But now, those same memories that had once reassured me were the ones that haunted me the most.

Could it be true? Had Anne and Earl Eric done something beyond the limits? Had they... had they been intimate before we were married? My stomach twisted at the thought, a sickening sensation that I couldn't shake.

The idea that Anne might have been involved with Earl Eric, that she might have been carrying his child all along, was too much to bear. But the more I tried to push the thought away, the more it clung to me, refusing to let go.

I reached the lodge and immediately poured myself a glass of whiskey, hoping it would help to steady my nerves. The burn of the alcohol did little to ease the tension in my chest, but I forced myself to take another sip, needing something—anything—to dull the pain.

Sitting alone in the dimly lit room, I found myself replaying every moment with Anne, every conversation, every touch, every glance. I had grown to care for her, to believe in the possibility of a real future together. But now, all of that was tainted by doubt. Had I been a fool? Had I been deceived from the start?

I wanted to believe that Anne was innocent, that the rumors were nothing more than malicious lies. But how could I be sure? What if the worst was true? What if the child she carried wasn't mine at all?

I couldn't ignore the nagging voice in the back of my mind that whispered that perhaps I had been naive. Perhaps I had been too eager to believe that this marriage, born of obligation and necessity, could become something more.

The thought that Anne might have betrayed me, that she might have been involved with Earl Eric before our marriage, left me feeling hollow. I didn't want to believe it—I wanted to trust her, to believe that what we had was real. But the doubt, once planted, was growing like a weed, threatening to choke everything else.

I downed the rest of the whiskey in one gulp, the burn doing nothing to chase away the cold dread that had settled in my chest. I had to confront Anne, to demand the truth, no matter how painful it might be. I couldn't live with this uncertainty, this gnawing fear that the life I thought we were building was based on a lie.

But even as I resolved to confront her, to demand answers, a part of me hesitated. What if she told me what I feared most? What if she admitted that the child wasn't mine, that she had been involved with Earl Eric all along? Could I bear to hear those words?

I sat there, staring into the empty glass, my mind a swirl of anger, doubt, and fear. I had wanted to believe in our marriage, in the future we were creating together. But now, all of that felt like it was crumbling around me, leaving nothing but the cold, hard reality of betrayal.

I didn't know what to believe anymore. The trust I had placed in Anne, in our future, had been shattered, and I was left with nothing but questions that had no easy answers.

And so, I sat in the silence of the lodge, wrestling with the doubts that threatened to consume me, knowing that nothing would ever be the same.

30

A Desperate Heart

Colin's absence was like a wound that wouldn't heal, a constant reminder of the rift that had opened between us. I had always feared that my lies would catch up to me, that the carefully constructed web I had woven would eventually unravel. But I hadn't anticipated how painful it would be when it finally happened.

Each day, I woke to an empty bed, the cold sheets beside me a stark contrast to the warmth we had once shared. Colin spent more and more time away from home, retreating to the lodge or immersing himself in work, leaving me alone with my thoughts and the heavy burden of guilt that weighed down on my heart.

I had wanted to be honest with him, to tell him the truth about the pregnancy that didn't exist, but the rumors had beaten me to it. Now, the truth seemed even more impossible to reveal. How could I confess everything when Colin already doubted me so deeply? How could I tell him that the baby he had grown so fond of, the future he had started to build in his mind, was nothing more than a lie?

But as the days passed, the fear of losing him grew stronger than my fear of the truth. I couldn't let him slip away, not now that I had realized how much he meant to me. I had to try to reach him, to make him see that what we had was worth fighting for, even if it was built on shaky ground.

One evening, after yet another day spent in lonely silence, I decided that I couldn't wait any longer. I had to talk to Colin, to make him listen to me. I found him in the study, sitting at his desk with a glass of whiskey in hand, his expression distant and cold.

"Colin," I began softly, stepping into the room. "We need to talk."

He didn't look up, his eyes fixed on the glass in front of him. "What is there to talk about, Anne?" His voice was flat, emotionless, as if he had already resigned himself to whatever outcome lay ahead.

"Please," I pleaded, moving closer. "I know things have been difficult, but I want to fix this. I want to make things right between us."

He finally looked up, his eyes meeting mine with a coldness that sent a shiver down my spine. "How do you propose we fix this, Anne? You can't even tell me the truth about these rumors. How can I believe anything you say?"

His words cut deep, but I forced myself to keep going. "I know I've made mistakes, and I'm sorry for that. But I care about you, Colin. I care about us. Can't we at least try to work through this together?"

He shook his head, the bitterness in his expression unmistakable. "Work through what, Anne? A marriage built on lies? A child that might not even be mine?" His voice rose with each word, the anger he had been holding back finally breaking through. "How can we work through something when I don't even know what's real anymore?"

I took a deep breath, trying to steady myself. "Colin, I promise you, the rumors are not true. I've never been with Earl Eric. The child—" I hesitated, the words catching in my throat. "The child is yours."

I bit my lip, why did I lie again. I should be honest now, but why can't I?

He stood up abruptly, his chair scraping against the floor. "Then prove it, Anne. Prove that you're telling the truth. Because right now, I don't know what to believe."

The challenge in his voice left me speechless. How could I prove something that wasn't true? How could I convince him of a lie that had already spun out of control?

Seeing my hesitation, Colin's expression hardened. "I thought so," he muttered, turning away from me. "You can't even defend yourself. What am

I supposed to do with that, Anne? How am I supposed to trust you?"

"Colin, please," I whispered, my voice trembling with desperation. "I love you. I know I've made mistakes, but I love you. Can't we find a way to move past this?"

He let out a bitter laugh, shaking his head. "Love, Anne? Is that what this is? Because it doesn't feel like love to me. It feels like deception, like manipulation."

Tears welled up in my eyes, but I blinked them back, refusing to let them fall. "I'm begging you, Colin. Don't shut me out. Let's talk about this, let's try to make this work."

But my pleas seemed to fall on deaf ears. He didn't respond, didn't even look at me. Instead, he walked past me, heading for the door without another word.

"Colin, please!" I called after him, my voice breaking. "Don't walk away from me!"

But he was already gone, the door closing behind him with a finality that echoed through the room.

I stood there, staring at the empty space where he had been, the tears finally spilling over. I had lost him. I could feel it in the cold emptiness that had settled in my chest, in the way he had looked at me with such disdain. The man I had come to love was slipping away from me, and there was nothing I could do to stop it.

Over the next few days, I tried everything I could think of to reach him. I left notes on his desk, asking him to meet me, to talk to me. I waited for him in the drawing room each evening, hoping that he would come home early, that he would sit with me by the fire like we used to. But each time, my efforts were met with silence, with coldness. He would come home late, retreat to his study without a word, or leave early in the morning before I even woke.

One night, I went to his study, determined to make him listen. I found him sitting at his desk, a familiar glass of whiskey in hand. I approached him cautiously, my heart pounding in my chest.

"Colin," I said softly, "I miss you. I miss us."

He didn't look up, his eyes fixed on the glass in front of him. "I don't know what you want from me, Anne," he replied, his voice distant. "I'm not sure there's anything left to miss."

I reached out, placing my hand over his, trying to bridge the gap between us. "There is, Colin. I know there is. Please, let's try to find our way back to each other."

He finally looked up, his eyes filled with a sadness that took my breath away. "I don't know if we can, Anne. Too much has happened."

"Please," I whispered, my voice trembling. "I love you."

For a moment, I thought I saw a flicker of something in his eyes, a glimmer of the connection we had once shared. But then, just as quickly, it was gone, replaced by that same cold distance.

"I need time," he said quietly, pulling his hand away from mine. "Time to figure out what's real and what isn't."

I nodded, tears welling up in my eyes once more. "I understand," I whispered, though my heart was breaking.

He didn't say anything more, just turned back to his desk, leaving me standing there, alone in the silence.

As I walked back to my room, the weight of everything pressed down on me like a heavy shroud. The love I had fought so hard to protect was slipping away, and I was powerless to stop it. All I could do was hope that, somehow, Colin would find it in his heart to forgive me, to give us another chance.

But as the days turned into weeks, and the distance between us grew even wider, I feared that I had lost him forever.

31

The Grip of Fear

The tension between Colin and me only deepened. The silence in Ashford Manor was suffocating, each day stretching into the next without the warmth of his presence. I had hoped that time would heal the wounds between us, that Colin would eventually come back to me, but the distance between us only seemed to grow. And as if the weight of our crumbling marriage wasn't enough, Earl Eric had begun his campaign of terror against me.

It started with the letters. They arrived at irregular intervals, each one more sinister than the last. At first, I had hoped they were simply the ramblings of a bitter man, still smarting from my rejection and marriage to Colin. But as the weeks went on, the tone of the letters grew darker, more threatening.

The first few letters were vague, filled with veiled threats and insinuations. Earl Eric hinted at the supposed secrets I was keeping, implying that he knew things about me that would ruin my reputation if they ever came to light. I tore each letter into pieces after reading it, refusing to let his words get to me. But as more letters arrived, the threats became more direct, more personal.

One letter in particular sent a chill down my spine:

"My dear Anne," it began, the words scrawled in a hand that seemed to vibrate with malice, **"I do hope you're enjoying your new life as the Marquess of Ashford's wife. I wonder how long that will last when he discovers the truth about you—about us. You see, I have friends in London, people who**

are very interested in hearing about your indiscretions. Imagine the scandal if they were to find out that the child you claim to carry isn't Colin's at all, but mine. You've made a powerful enemy in me, Anne, and I will see you brought to your knees."**

My hands trembled as I read the letter, the words blurring in front of my eyes. Earl Eric was more than just angry—he was vengeful, and he wouldn't stop until he had destroyed me. The thought of him spreading these lies about me, of society believing that I had been unfaithful, was terrifying. But what scared me even more was the possibility that Colin might believe him too.

If Colin already doubted me, what would he think if these rumors spread further? Would he finally give up on us entirely, convinced that everything we had was a lie?

I felt trapped, cornered by the lies I had spun and the threats that now surrounded me. Each time a letter arrived, I was filled with a sickening dread, afraid to open it yet unable to ignore it. The worst part was that I had no one to turn to—no one I could confide in without exposing my own lies. If I told anyone the truth, it would unravel everything, and the little hope I had left would be gone.

I considered going to Colin, confessing everything in a desperate bid to salvage our marriage. But I knew that if I did, it would only confirm his worst fears. He would hate me, not just for deceiving him, but for dragging him into a scandal that could ruin both of us.

I even thought about confiding in Adelaide, my sister, who had always been my confidante. But how could I tell her the truth? How could I admit that I had fabricated a pregnancy, that I had trapped her best friend into a marriage based on lies? It would destroy her trust in me, and I couldn't bear the thought of losing her too.

I was alone, utterly and completely alone, with no way out of the mess I had created. I couldn't turn to anyone, couldn't ask for help without risking everything. The walls were closing in, and I could feel the noose tightening around my neck with each passing day.

The nights were the worst. Alone in my room, I would lie awake for hours, my mind racing with thoughts of what might happen if Earl Eric made good on his threats. I could picture the scandal erupting, the whispers behind my back, the cold looks from those who had once called me friend. And worst of all, I could see Colin's face, twisted with disgust and betrayal as he finally learned the truth.

I knew I had to do something, but what? How could I fight against a man as ruthless and determined as Earl Eric? I had no power, no influence, nothing to use against him. All I had were my lies, and those were quickly unraveling.

I began to avoid the staff at Ashford Manor, afraid that they might sense something was wrong. I stayed in my room as much as possible, only emerging for meals or when I knew Colin wouldn't be around. The more isolated I became, the more the fear took hold, wrapping around me like a vise that wouldn't let go.

One evening, after receiving yet another letter from Earl Eric, I finally broke down. I couldn't keep this up, couldn't continue pretending that everything was fine when my world was falling apart. I needed help, needed someone to tell me what to do. But the only person I could think of was Colin, and he was the last person I could confide in.

Tears streamed down my face as I sat at my vanity, the latest letter crumpled in my hand. I felt like I was drowning, the weight of everything pressing down on me until I couldn't breathe. The guilt, the fear, the loneliness—it was all too much. I wanted to scream, to tear the letters to shreds and burn them so they could never haunt me again.

But instead, I just sat there, paralyzed by the enormity of what I had done and what I was facing. Earl Eric had me cornered, and I had no way out.

The only thing I could do was try to hold on, to survive each day as it came, and hope that somehow, some way, this nightmare would end before it destroyed me. But as the days stretched into weeks, I began to lose hope that there would be any escape at all.

32

A Fragile Hope

Visiting Adelaide should have brought me some comfort, but as I made my way to Lightwood Manor, I couldn't shake the heavy weight of dread that had settled in my chest. The lies, the threats, and the distance between Colin and me had taken a toll on my body and spirit. I felt worn down, as if the very essence of who I was had been slowly chipped away over the past few weeks.

When I arrived, I was greeted warmly by the staff and led to Adelaide's chambers. The room was filled with soft light filtering through the curtains, and the air was sweet with the scent of fresh flowers. Adelaide sat in an overstuffed armchair, her hands resting on the gentle curve of her belly. She looked serene, her face glowing with the happiness that comes from expecting a child, but there was a hint of exhaustion in her eyes that I couldn't ignore.

"Anne!" she exclaimed, a wide smile spreading across her face as she saw me. "It's so good to see you."

I forced a smile, trying to mask the turmoil I was feeling inside. "And you, Adelaide. You're looking well."

Adelaide chuckled softly, rubbing her belly. "Well enough, though Bastian has practically confined me to this room. He's convinced I'll go into labor any minute now, and he won't hear of me leaving the manor. I suppose he's just worried."

I nodded, taking a seat beside her. "He's right to be cautious. You're so close now."

She sighed, her smile fading slightly as she studied me. "But enough about me. What about you, Anne? You look pale. Is everything all right? Is it the pregnancy?"

The question made my heart skip a beat, and I felt a pang of guilt. I wasn't pregnant, but Adelaide didn't know that. I couldn't tell her the truth, not now, not when she was so close to giving birth and needed to remain calm and healthy. The last thing I wanted was to burden her with my troubles.

"Yes," I replied softly, lowering my gaze. "I've been feeling a bit unwell lately. Morning sickness, I suppose. I've had some fever too, and no appetite. But it's nothing to worry about."

Adelaide's brow furrowed with concern. "Anne, you should take care of yourself. Pregnancy can be hard on the body, especially in the early stages. Are you sure you're all right?"

I nodded, forcing another smile. "I'm fine, Adelaide. Really. It's just a bit overwhelming sometimes, that's all."

She reached out and took my hand, her grip gentle but firm. "If you ever need anything, Anne, you know you can come to me. I'm always here for you."

Her words, so full of love and support, made my chest tighten with emotion. I wanted to tell her everything, to spill the truth about Earl Eric's threats, about my strained relationship with Colin, about the lies that were slowly suffocating me. But I couldn't. Not now. Not when Adelaide needed to focus on her own health and the impending birth of her child.

"Thank you," I whispered, squeezing her hand. "It means a lot to me."

We sat in silence for a moment, the unspoken words hanging heavily between us. I could see that Adelaide was worried, that she sensed something was wrong, but she didn't press me further. Instead, she offered me a soft smile, her eyes filled with understanding.

Just as I was about to say something, the door to the room opened, and Colin stepped inside. The sight of him made my heart leap, a mixture of relief and anxiety flooding through me.

"Colin," Adelaide said warmly, her face lighting up. "It's good to see you."

He smiled, but it was a shadow of the smile I used to know. "I just wanted to make sure you were all right," he said, his gaze shifting to me briefly before returning to Adelaide. "How are you feeling?"

"Impatient," Adelaide replied with a laugh. "But otherwise fine. Bastian's been hovering over me like a mother hen."

Colin chuckled softly, the sound bringing a brief warmth to the room. "He means well. He just wants to make sure everything goes smoothly."

As they spoke, I couldn't help but steal glances at Colin. He looked tired, worn down by everything that had happened between us, but there was a moment—a fleeting one—when our eyes met, and I saw something familiar in his gaze. It wasn't the coldness I had grown accustomed to, nor the anger that had driven us apart. It was something softer, something that reminded me of the man I had fallen for, even if I hadn't meant to.

It was brief, but it was enough to give me a glimmer of hope that maybe—just maybe—things between us weren't completely beyond repair.

Colin's attention returned to Adelaide, and he spoke to her with the care and concern of an older brother. I watched them, feeling like an outsider in the warmth of their exchange, yet grateful for the rare moment of connection I had felt with him.

After a few more minutes of conversation, Colin turned to me, his expression more guarded than before. "Anne, how are you feeling?" he asked, his voice neutral.

I hesitated, unsure of how to answer. I wanted to tell him everything, to open up about the fear and guilt that had been eating away at me, but I couldn't. Not here. Not now.

"I'm managing," I replied softly, my eyes searching his for any sign of the warmth I had glimpsed earlier. "Thank you for asking."

He nodded, but the conversation didn't go any further. Instead, he turned back to Adelaide, discussing the arrangements for her care in the coming weeks. I listened quietly, trying to ignore the ache in my chest, the longing for things to be different between us.

When it was time for us to leave, Adelaide hugged me tightly, her belly pressing against mine in a way that made my heart ache even more. "Take care of yourself, Anne," she whispered. "And remember, I'm always here for you."

"Thank you, Adelaide," I whispered back, blinking back tears. "You take care too."

We walked together to the door, his presence both comforting and painful. As we reached the entrance, I turned to him, hoping for something—anything—that might reassure me that our marriage wasn't completely lost.

"Colin," I began, my voice trembling slightly, "I... I'm glad you picked me up today."

He looked at me, his expression unreadable. "Me too, Anne," he said quietly. But there was a distance in his voice, a barrier that I couldn't breach.

As our carriage walked away from Lightwood Manor, the glimmer of hope I had felt began to fade, replaced by the cold reality of our situation. The warmth between us had been brief, a fleeting moment in the midst of a storm that still raged around us.

But even that small moment was enough to keep me going, to give me the strength to face whatever lay ahead. For now, I would hold on to that hope, fragile as it was, and pray that somehow, some way, we could find our way back to each other.

33

The Internal Struggle

The carriage jolted slightly as it began the journey back to Ashford Manor, the rhythmic clatter of hooves on the cobblestones filling the tense silence between Anne and me. We sat across from each other, the space between us feeling like a chasm that neither of us could cross. I stole a glance at her, noticing how pale and exhausted she looked, her usual vivacity drained away.

It was a sharp contrast to the woman I had married—a woman who had always seemed so composed, so sure of herself. But now, as she sat quietly in the carriage, her hands folded in her lap, I could see the weight of our situation pressing down on her, much like it was on me. There was something in her eyes, a weariness, a dawning realization of the consequences of her actions. It was as if she finally understood the damage that had been done, not just to me, but to herself as well.

The lies, the deception—they had created a wall between us, one that seemed impossible to break down. And yet, despite everything, I found myself struggling with my own feelings. The anger that had driven me to distance myself from her was still there, but so was something else. Something that made me look at her and see more than just the woman who had trapped me in this marriage.

I couldn't deny the growing conflict within me. Despite the lies, despite the scandal with Earl Eric, I was still drawn to her. There was a part of me that wanted to reach out, to bridge the gap between us, to find a way to heal the wounds that had been inflicted. But that same part of me was frustrated—frustrated that I still cared, that I couldn't simply shut her out and move on.

I glanced at Anne again, her pale face turned toward the window, her expression distant. She was pregnant—or so I believed—and her condition must have been affecting her more than I realized. The thought made my chest tighten with a mix of concern and guilt. Whatever had happened between us, whatever lies had been told, she was still carrying what I thought was our child. She was still the woman I had vowed to protect, and seeing her like this made it impossible to ignore the instinct to care for her.

That was why I had come to Lightwood Manor to pick her up, even though I knew she could have returned on her own. I told myself it was because of her pregnancy, that she shouldn't be making the journey alone, but deep down, I knew it was more than that. It was the worry gnawing at me, the sense that something was wrong, something beyond the scandal that had thrown our lives into disarray.

"Anne," I finally said, breaking the silence, my voice softer than I intended. She turned to look at me, her eyes wide and almost startled, as if she hadn't expected me to speak.

"Yes?" she replied, her voice barely above a whisper.

I hesitated, the words caught in my throat. I wanted to ask if she was all right, if there was something she wasn't telling me, but the fear of what her answer might be held me back. Instead, I settled for something safer, something that wouldn't force us to confront the truth.

"I noticed you weren't feeling well earlier," I said, my eyes scanning her face for any signs of what might be wrong. "Is there anything I can do to help?"

Her expression softened, and for a moment, I saw a flicker of the warmth that had once existed between us. But then it was gone, replaced by a resigned sadness. "I'm fine, Colin," she answered quietly, though the exhaustion in her voice betrayed her words. "It's just... everything has been overwhelming lately. I'm sorry if I've caused you any trouble."

I frowned, the apology catching me off guard. Anne had always been so strong, so determined, that hearing her sound so defeated was unsettling. "You don't have to apologize," I said, my frustration ebbing slightly. "I just want to make sure you're taking care of yourself, especially now."

Her gaze dropped to her lap, her fingers nervously twisting the fabric of her dress. "I'm trying," she murmured. "But it's hard when... when things are like this between us."

There it was—the admission of the rift that had formed, the unspoken acknowledgment that we were both struggling under the weight of what had happened. I should have been relieved that she recognized it, but instead, it only made the knot in my chest tighten.

"I know," I said, my voice strained. "I know things aren't easy right now, but that doesn't mean we can't try to make them better."

She looked up at me then, her eyes shining with a mixture of hope and fear. "Do you really think we can?" she asked, her voice trembling. "After everything that's happened... do you really think there's a way to fix this?"

I wanted to say yes, to reassure her that we could find our way back to each other, but the words wouldn't come. The truth was, I didn't know. I didn't know if we could rebuild the trust that had been shattered, or if the feelings I had for her were strong enough to overcome the lies that had torn us apart.

"I don't know," I admitted, my voice barely audible. "But I think it's worth trying. For both our sakes."

Her eyes searched mine, and for a moment, I thought I saw the flicker of something—maybe understanding, maybe hope. But it was fleeting, and soon her gaze dropped once more.

The rest of the journey passed in silence, the tension between us thick and palpable. I couldn't stop thinking about the look in her eyes, the way she had seemed so fragile, so uncertain. It was a side of Anne I had never seen before, and it only added to the confusion I felt.

When we finally arrived at Ashford Manor, I helped her out of the carriage, my hand lingering on hers for just a moment longer than necessary. She looked up at me, and there it was again—that flicker of something I couldn't quite place.

"Thank you," she said softly, her voice filled with a sincerity that made my heart ache.

I nodded, unable to find the right words to respond. As we walked inside, I couldn't shake the feeling that things were shifting between us, that the walls we had built were beginning to crack. But whether that was a good thing or not, I didn't know.

All I knew was that despite everything, despite the anger, the doubt, and the lies, I still cared for her. And that scared me more than anything.

34

The Breaking Point

The grand ballroom was a swirl of color and sound, the clinking of glasses and the murmur of polite conversation filling the air as London's elite mingled beneath the glittering chandeliers. It was a night like any other, one of countless social events that had become a fixture in our lives. But tonight, there was an undercurrent of tension that I couldn't shake, a sense of foreboding that made my heart race with anxiety.

I stood near the edge of the room, my hands clasped tightly together, trying to steady myself as I exchanged pleasantries with the guests who drifted by. Colin was somewhere in the crowd, but I hadn't seen him for some time. His absence only added to my unease. We had been distant lately, more so than usual, and I knew that the rumors surrounding me had reached a fever pitch.

Earl Eric was here tonight, his presence a dark shadow that loomed over me. I had seen him earlier, moving through the crowd with that same smug smile that always made my skin crawl. He had yet to approach me, but I knew it was only a matter of time. He thrived on chaos, on the destruction of reputations, and I was his favorite target.

As the night wore on, I found myself gravitating toward the edges of the room, avoiding the more crowded areas where the stares and whispers seemed to follow me. I felt like an outsider in a world that had once been my own, the walls closing in as the weight of my lies pressed down on me.

It was then that I saw him—Earl Eric—moving toward me with that predatory grace that always made me uneasy. He was dressed impeccably, his dark eyes gleaming with a malicious intent that sent a shiver down my spine.

"Lady Ashford," he greeted me with a mocking bow, his voice dripping with false courtesy. "You're looking rather pale this evening. Is something the matter?"

I forced a smile, trying to maintain my composure. "I'm quite well, thank you," I replied, my voice steady despite the dread that curled in my stomach.

He chuckled, the sound low and menacing. "I must say, it's quite impressive how you've managed to maintain such poise in the face of... certain rumors. One might almost believe that there's no truth to them at all."

My heart skipped a beat, the thinly veiled threat in his words cutting through me like a knife. He was toying with me, baiting me, and I could feel the eyes of those around us beginning to turn in our direction. The air in the room seemed to grow colder, the whispers louder, as if everyone was waiting for the inevitable explosion.

Before I could respond, a voice cut through the tension like a blade. "Eric."

I turned to see Colin standing just behind me, his face a mask of barely controlled fury. His eyes locked onto Earl Eric's with a burning intensity that made my breath catch in my throat.

"Colin," Earl Eric greeted him with a smirk, clearly enjoying the tension he was creating. "I was just having a lovely chat with your wife."

Colin's gaze shifted to me, and for a moment, I saw something raw and pained in his eyes—something that sent a fresh wave of guilt crashing over me. But it was gone as quickly as it had appeared, replaced by a cold, steely resolve.

"I'm not interested in your games tonight, Eric," Colin said, his voice tight. "Leave Anne alone."

Earl Eric raised an eyebrow, clearly amused by Colin's anger. "Games? I'm merely making conversation. Though I must admit, it is fascinating how rumors seem to follow some people, no matter where they go."

The insinuation was clear, and I felt the ground shift beneath me as the room seemed to close in. Colin's fists clenched at his sides, his jaw tightening as he fought to keep his composure. But I could see the cracks forming, the control slipping.

"Enough," Colin said, his voice low and dangerous. "If you have something to say, say it. Otherwise, I suggest you keep your mouth shut."

Earl Eric's smile widened, a predator toying with its prey. "Very well, then. I'll be blunt. Tell me, Colin—have you ever wondered if the child your wife claims to be carrying is really yours?"

The words hung in the air like a death sentence, the silence that followed deafening. I felt the blood drain from my face, my vision narrowing as the world seemed to tilt around me. The room was spinning, the stares of the guests burning into my skin as my worst fears were laid bare for all to see.

Colin's reaction was immediate and explosive. "How dare you," he snarled, stepping forward as if he intended to strike Earl Eric right then and there. "How dare you spread such vile lies?"

But Earl Eric didn't back down. If anything, he looked even more pleased with himself, as if he had just played the winning hand in a game he had been planning for a long time. "Lies?" he echoed, feigning innocence. "I merely asked a question. After all, where there's smoke, there's usually fire."

Colin turned to me, his expression torn between rage and desperation. "Anne," he said, his voice trembling with barely restrained emotion. "Tell me it's not true. Tell me these rumors are nothing but lies."

I opened my mouth to speak, but no sound came out. I could feel the walls closing in, the weight of everyone's eyes on me, the whispers that seemed to grow louder with each passing second. My mind raced, searching for the words that would make everything right, that would dispel the doubts and fears that had taken root in Colin's heart.

But I couldn't find them. The lies, the deception—they had woven such a tangled web that I couldn't see a way out. All I could do was stand there, my silence a damning confirmation of the worst fears I knew Colin had been harboring.

"Anne," Colin said again, more insistently this time, his voice breaking. "For God's sake, say something."

But still, I couldn't. I was paralyzed by the enormity of what was happening, by the realization that this moment, this confrontation, was the culmination of everything I had feared. The tension between us, the distance that had grown wider with each passing day—it had all led to this, to a public reckoning that I was powerless to stop.

The room was spinning, the stares and whispers growing louder, more oppressive. I felt like I was suffocating, drowning in the weight of my own lies. And then, as if from a great distance, I heard Colin's voice again—only this time, it was cold, detached, as if he had finally reached the breaking point.

"I can't do this," he said, his words like a knife to my heart. "I can't keep pretending that everything is fine when it's not."

With that, he turned and walked away, leaving me standing there, alone and exposed. The whispers followed him, a murmur of disbelief and judgment that seemed to close in around me like a noose.

I watched him go, my heart shattering into a million pieces as the reality of what had just happened hit me with full force. I had lost him. I had driven him away with my lies, with my inability to face the truth. And now, I was left to face the consequences alone.

The room seemed to close in on me, the walls pressing down as the stares and whispers grew louder, more insistent. I could see Adelaide and Duke Bastian across the room, their expressions a mix of concern and helplessness. They had seen everything, heard everything, but there was nothing they could do to help me now.

The whispers turned into a low buzz, and I felt as though the walls were closing in, suffocating me with the weight of my own disgrace. I had to get out of there. I couldn't stay in that room, couldn't bear the judgmental eyes on me any longer. The pain was too much, the humiliation too raw.

Without another thought, I gathered my skirts and hurried out of the ballroom, my heart pounding in my chest. I didn't know where I was going, only that I had to find Colin, that I had to make this right before it was too late.

I heard footsteps behind me, quick and insistent, and then Adelaide's voice calling my name, but I couldn't stop. I couldn't turn back now, not when everything was slipping through my fingers.

I ran through the corridors, my vision blurred with tears, my breath coming in short, ragged gasps. The walls seemed to close in around me, the air thick and suffocating as I searched for any sign of Colin. I couldn't lose him—not like this. Not after everything we had been through.

Finally, I spotted him in the distance, his figure dark against the dim light of the hallway. He was moving quickly, his strides long and purposeful as if he was determined to get as far away from me as possible.

"Colin!" I called out, my voice cracking with desperation.

He didn't stop. If anything, he quickened his pace, as if he couldn't bear to hear another word from me. But I couldn't let him go—not like this. Not without trying to make him understand.

"Colin, please!" I cried, my voice echoing off the walls as I ran after him.

He reached the entrance to the manor, his hand on the door, ready to push it open and disappear into the night. But I reached him just in time, grabbing his arm, my fingers digging into the fabric of his jacket as I tried to pull him back.

"Don't leave," I whispered, my voice trembling. "Please, Colin. Don't leave me like this."

He turned to face me, and the look in his eyes broke my heart all over again. There was so much pain there, so much hurt and betrayal that I couldn't even begin to fathom. He was struggling, just as much as I was, but in that moment, I knew that the damage I had done might be too great to repair.

"I can't do this, Anne," he said, his voice low and strained. "I can't keep living like this, not knowing what's true and what's a lie."

"I'm sorry," I choked out, my tears falling freely now. "I'm so sorry, Colin. I never meant for it to get this far. I never meant to hurt you."

He looked at me for a long moment, his expression unreadable. Then, with a deep, shuddering breath, he shook his head. "But you did, Anne. You did."

I felt my grip on his arm loosen, my heart breaking as I realized the depth of the chasm between us. I had thought that I could control this, that I could fix it somehow. But I was wrong. I had pushed him too far, and now there was no going back.

"Colin," I whispered, my voice barely audible. "Please, let me try to make it right. Let me try to fix this."

He closed his eyes, his jaw clenching as he fought to keep his emotions in check. "I don't know if that's possible anymore," he said quietly, the pain in his voice cutting through me like a knife.

For a moment, we stood there in silence, the weight of everything that had happened hanging between us like a heavy shroud. I could feel him slipping away, feel the love we had once shared crumbling beneath the weight of my lies. And yet, I couldn't let go. I couldn't let him go.

"Please," I whispered again, my voice breaking. "Please don't leave me."

He opened his eyes, and for a brief moment, I saw the flicker of something—regret, sorrow, love?—but it was gone as quickly as it had appeared. He gently pulled his arm free from my grasp, his expression a mixture of resignation and heartbreak.

35

The Reckoning

I couldn't let it end like this. The thought of losing Colin forever without knowing the truth, was unbearable. "Colin, wait!" I cried, my voice breaking. "Please listen to me!"

"What more is there to say, Anne?"

I stood there, breathless and trembling, the weight of what I was about to do pressing down on me like a leaden blanket. I knew that this was my last chance—my only chance—to make things right. But I also knew that what I was about to confess could destroy whatever fragile connection we still had.

"I have to tell you the truth," I began, my voice shaking. "I can't keep lying to you, but not anymore. You deserve to know everything."

Colin's eyes narrowed, his jaw tightening as he waited for me to continue. The silence between us was suffocating, the tension so thick that it felt like it was choking me. But I couldn't turn back now. I had to do this, no matter the cost.

"I'm not pregnant," I said, the words tumbling out in a rush, as if I feared I might lose my nerve if I didn't say them quickly. "I never was. I lied about it, Colin. I lied to trap you into marrying me."

The words hung in the air, heavy and damning, and I watched as Colin's expression shifted from anger to shock, and then to something darker, something more dangerous. His fists clenched at his sides, and for a moment, I thought he might strike out, but he remained rooted to the spot, his eyes boring into mine.

"What?" he whispered, his voice laced with disbelief. "What did you just say?"

Tears welled up in my eyes, but I forced myself to keep going. "I was desperate," I continued, my voice cracking under the weight of my confession. "Earl Eric proposed to me, and I couldn't bear the thought of marrying him. I saw no way out, and I thought... I thought if I could just make you marry me, everything would be okay."

Colin's face twisted with rage, his eyes flashing with a fury that sent a chill down my spine. "You thought you could manipulate me? That you could lie to me about something as important as a child?" His voice was low, dangerous, each word seething with controlled anger.

"It was wrong, I know it was wrong," I sobbed, my hands trembling as I reached out to him, desperate for any sign of forgiveness. "But I didn't know what else to do. I was scared, and I didn't want to lose you. And then... then I fell in love with you, Colin. Truly, deeply. And I knew I had made a terrible mistake, but I didn't know how to fix it."

Colin recoiled as if I had struck him, his eyes wide with a mix of horror and disbelief. "You fell in love with me?" he spat, his voice thick with scorn. "After you lied to me, after you trapped me in this farce of a marriage, now you want to talk about love?"

I nodded, the tears spilling over and streaking down my cheeks. "Yes, Colin, I do. I know it's too late, and I know I've ruined everything, but it's the truth. I love you, and I'm so sorry for everything I've done."

He stared at me, his chest heaving with the effort to contain his rage. "You're sorry?" he repeated, his voice trembling with fury. "Sorry doesn't begin to cover it, Anne. You've taken everything from me—my trust, my hopes for the future—and you want to tell me you're sorry?"

"Please, Colin," I begged, my voice breaking. "Please, don't walk away from me. I'll do anything to make this right. I'll do anything to earn your forgiveness."

But he wasn't listening. The fury in his eyes was too intense, too consuming. With a harsh, bitter laugh, he shook his head, turning away from me as if he couldn't bear to look at me any longer.

"I need to get out of here," he muttered, his voice tight. "I need to get as far away from you as possible."

"Colin, no!" I cried, reaching out to grab his arm, but he shook me off, his expression twisted with anger and pain.

"You've done enough damage, Anne," he said coldly, his eyes narrowing. "I don't want to see you right now. I don't even want to think about you. I need space, and I need to figure out what the hell I'm going to do now."

He turned on his heel and began to walk away, his footsteps echoing in the stillness of the night. I watched him go, my heart breaking with every step he took, knowing that I had just destroyed the one thing I had been trying so desperately to save.

But before I could even begin to process the depth of my despair, I heard a scream—a scream that cut through the night air like a knife.

"Anne!" It was Adelaide's voice, filled with pain and panic. I turned to see her clutching her swollen belly, her face pale and twisted with agony as she collapsed to the ground.

"Adelaide!" I cried, rushing to her side as Duke Bastian hurried over from where he had been trying to catch up to us. His face was a mask of fear and determination as he knelt beside her, his hands steady as he supported her.

"She's in labor," Bastian said urgently, his eyes flicking to mine with a mixture of concern and command. "We need to get her inside, now."

36

A Night of Shadows and Screams

My mind was reeling, the emotions of the last few minutes crashing into the new wave of panic as I watched my sister writhe in pain. I was still in shock from my confrontation with Colin, but there was no time to think, no time to process. I had to act.

Together, Bastian and I lifted Adelaide, carrying her as quickly and gently as we could back toward the manor. Her screams of pain echoed in my ears, each one a reminder of how everything was unraveling around me. The love I had confessed, the lies I had exposed—they all seemed distant now, overshadowed by the immediate crisis at hand.

Colin was gone. My marriage was in shambles. But right now, all that mattered was getting Adelaide the help she needed, to see her safely through this terrifying moment.

As we reached the manor and hurried inside, the weight of my actions pressed down on me with a crushing force. I had confessed everything to Colin, and now I feared I had lost him forever. The last remnants of hope slipped through my fingers as I realized that the damage might be beyond repair.

As we rushed Adelaide to her chambers, her screams of pain echoing through the halls of the manor like a haunting refrain. My heart pounded with fear and guilt, each beat a painful reminder of how I had failed my sister. The confrontation with Colin was already a distant memory, swallowed by the immediate terror of watching Adelaide in the throes of a difficult labor.

Once we reached her room, the midwife and the physician quickly took charge, directing us to lay Adelaide on the bed, where she continued to writhe in agony, clutching her swollen belly. Her face was pale, beads of sweat standing out on her forehead as she gasped for breath between the cries of pain.

"Anne," Adelaide whimpered, reaching out for me with trembling hands.

"I'm here, Adelaide," I whispered, grabbing her hand and holding it tightly. I could barely contain the tears that threatened to spill over. "I'm right here. You're going to be okay."

But even as I said the words, I could see the fear in her eyes, the terror that mirrored my own. Her labor had come too soon, likely brought on by the shock of what she had witnessed. The pain seemed unbearable, and I could do nothing but hold her hand and pray.

The room was a whirlwind of activity as the midwife prepared for the delivery. The physician hovered nearby, his expression grim as he instructed the servants to fetch more hot water and clean linens. The air was thick with the scent of blood and sweat, and the sounds of Adelaide's screams pierced through me like a knife.

Hours passed in a blur of pain and fear. Adelaide's screams grew louder, more desperate, as she struggled to bring the baby into the world. I stayed by her side, whispering words of encouragement, even though my own heart was breaking with each cry of pain.

"It's going to be all right, Adelaide," I repeated over and over, even as I felt the weight of my own guilt pressing down on me. "You're going to be all right."

But it wasn't all right. The labor was difficult—far more difficult than any of us had anticipated. The baby wasn't coming, and the midwife's face grew more and more worried as the hours dragged on. Adelaide's screams became more frantic, her grip on my hand tightening to the point of pain, but I didn't dare pull away. I couldn't leave her, not now, not when she needed me the most.

At one point, the midwife shook her head and looked at me with grim determination. "It's not good," she whispered, her voice low enough that Adelaide couldn't hear. "The baby is stuck. If it doesn't come soon..."

Her words trailed off, but the meaning was clear. My breath caught in my throat as I fought back a wave of panic. I knew that childbirth was dangerous, that it claimed the lives of many women, but I had never imagined that Adelaide might be one of them. The thought of losing her, of watching her slip away because of something I had caused, was too much to bear.

I could see the same fear in Duke Bastian's eyes whenever I stepped out to update him. He paced the hallway like a caged animal, his face pale and drawn with worry. Each time I emerged from the room, he would rush over, his voice tight with anxiety.

"Is she all right? Is the baby all right?" he would ask, his eyes searching mine for any hint of reassurance.

"She's still struggling," I would reply, trying to keep my voice steady. "But she's strong, Bastian. She'll make it through this."

He would nod, but I could see the terror in his eyes, the helplessness that mirrored my own. At one point, he grabbed my arm, his grip desperate. "Anne, if it comes to it... if they have to choose..."

I froze, the implication of his words hitting me like a blow. I had known this was a possibility, but hearing him say it out loud made it all too real. My heart clenched with fear, but I knew what he was going to say before he said it.

"Adelaide is the priority," he whispered, his voice breaking. "If they have to choose between her and the baby... save Adelaide."

I nodded, unable to speak. The thought of losing my sister was unbearable, but I knew that Duke Bastian's love for her was even deeper than my own. He couldn't lose her, not like this.

Back in the room, the midwife and the physician continued their work, their faces etched with concentration. Adelaide's screams had become hoarse, her strength waning as the hours wore on. I stayed by her side, wiping the sweat from her brow, whispering words of comfort, even as my own heart broke with every cry of pain.

"Anne," Adelaide gasped, her eyes wild with fear and pain. "I can't... I can't do this..."

"Yes, you can," I whispered fiercely, clutching her hand as if I could somehow transfer my strength to her. "You can, Adelaide. You're the strongest person I know. Just a little longer, please."

She squeezed my hand, her grip weakening, and I could see the exhaustion in her eyes, the desperation. But she nodded, trusting me, holding on because I told her she could.

Finally, after what felt like an eternity, the midwife's voice rang out with a note of hope. "I can see the head! Push, my lady, push with all you have left!"

Adelaide's grip tightened on my hand, her face contorted with pain as she summoned every ounce of strength she had left. The room was filled with tension, everyone holding their breath as we waited, hoping, praying that this would be the final push.

And then, with one last, agonizing cry, the baby came. There was a moment of silence—a heartbeat of pure terror—before the room was filled with the sound of a baby's wail, strong and clear. The tension broke, replaced by a wave of relief so intense that I felt my knees buckle beneath me.

"He's here," the midwife said, her voice choked with emotion as she lifted the baby for us to see. "A healthy baby boy."

Tears streamed down my face as I looked at Adelaide, her face pale and drenched with sweat, but alive. Alive and breathing. The baby was placed in her arms, his cries filling the room as she held him close, her expression one of exhausted joy.

"You did it, Adelaide," I whispered, my voice thick with emotion. "You did it."

She looked up at me, her eyes filled with tears, and for a moment, we just held each other's gaze, sisters bound by the terror and relief of the moment. Then she looked down at her son, her face softening with love as she cradled him against her chest.

"Thank you," she whispered, her voice so faint that I barely heard it. "Thank you for being here with me."

I could only nod, too overwhelmed to speak. My heart was heavy with guilt, knowing that I had played a part in the events that had brought us to this point. But in that moment, all that mattered was that Adelaide was safe, and her son was in her arms.

Duke Bastian burst into the room, his face a mixture of fear and hope as he rushed to Adelaide's side. When he saw the baby, his expression broke into one of pure joy, and he reached out to touch his son, his hand trembling.

"You're all right," he whispered, his voice thick with emotion as he leaned down to kiss Adelaide's forehead. "You're both all right."

Adelaide smiled up at him, her face radiant with love and relief. "We're all right, Bastian. We're all right."

I watched them together, my heart aching with a mixture of happiness and sorrow. They were a family now, whole and complete, while my own marriage was in shambles, shattered by the weight of my lies.

But as I looked at the new life that had just entered the world, I felt a flicker of hope. Perhaps, in time, there could be healing. Perhaps there was still a chance to make things right.

But for now, I was content to watch my sister, her husband, and their son as they basked in the glow of their new family. The future was uncertain, but this moment—this precious, fragile moment—was filled with a peace that I would cling to in the days to come.

37

The Absence

The first few days after that night were a blur of anger and disbelief. I couldn't get Anne's confession out of my mind—the lies she had told, the way she had manipulated me into this marriage. It was as though my world had been turned upside down, and all I could feel was the cold, bitter sting of betrayal.

I didn't want to see her. I didn't want to hear her voice, to look into those eyes that had once seemed so full of sincerity but had been hiding so much. She wasn't welcome at Ashford Manor anymore, and the thought of her presence made my skin crawl. So, when I realized she hadn't returned to the manor after that night, I felt nothing but a hollow relief.

Let her stay away, I told myself. Let her be with Adelaide or at her parents' house. I didn't care. The less I saw of her, the better. She could stay gone for all I cared.

But as the days passed, the silence in the manor became more pronounced, the emptiness more unsettling. I noticed her absence, of course, but I told myself it was a good thing. A reprieve from the turmoil she had caused. I tried to immerse myself in my work, to distract myself with the endless responsibilities that came with managing the estate. But no matter how hard I tried, I couldn't shake the feeling that something was off.

Adelaide had given birth, I heard. A healthy baby boy. The news reached me through a letter from Duke Bastian, brief and to the point, as was his style. There was no mention of Anne in the letter, but I assumed she was with her sister, helping care for the newborn. It made sense, and I pushed any lingering thoughts of her absence to the back of my mind.

But then a week passed, and she still didn't return. The manor felt even emptier, the silence more oppressive. The servants moved through the halls with an uneasy air, as if they too felt the weight of her absence. I found myself waiting for her, half-expecting her to walk through the door with some explanation, some excuse. But she didn't come.

The thought of her staying away didn't bring the satisfaction I expected. Instead, it left a gnawing unease in my chest, a discomfort that grew with each passing day. It wasn't just that she wasn't here—it was the fact that she was nowhere. No one had seen her, no one knew where she was, and that thought began to fester in my mind.

Where was she? Why hadn't she returned to Ashford Manor or even her parents' house? The longer she stayed away, the more the worry grew, creeping into my thoughts at the most unexpected times. But I shoved it down, stubbornly clinging to my anger, to the righteous indignation I felt at her betrayal. She had lied to me, trapped me in a marriage I hadn't wanted, and now she was hiding. It was what she deserved.

Or so I kept telling myself.

By the time the second week of her disappearance rolled around, that gnawing worry had transformed into full-blown panic. I tried to tell myself that I didn't care, that she wasn't my responsibility, but the truth was, I did care. I cared too much, and it was driving me mad.

Where was she?

On the fourteenth day, I couldn't take it anymore. I rode out to her parents' house, fully expecting to find her there, hiding away from the world. Perhaps she had decided to stay with them out of shame, or maybe she was waiting for me to come to her. I didn't know, but I was determined to find out.

The ride to the Earl of Windermere's estate was long and tense. My thoughts were a chaotic mess, veering wildly between anger, fear, and something I refused to name—something that felt a lot like guilt. I didn't want to admit that I might have driven her away, that my rejection had hurt her so deeply that she couldn't bring herself to return. But the thought gnawed at me all the same.

When I arrived at the estate, I was met by a servant who informed me that the Earl and Countess were away. I didn't care about that—I only cared about finding Anne.

"Where is Lady Ashford?" I demanded, my voice sharper than I intended. "I need to speak with her."

The servant looked confused, his brow furrowing as he tried to make sense of my request. "Lady Ashford, my lord? I'm afraid she's not here."

I stared at him, the words not registering at first. "What do you mean she's not here? Where is she?"

"I don't know, my lord," he replied, looking genuinely concerned now. "Lady Ashford hasn't been here for some time. We haven't seen her."

A cold wave of dread washed over me, leaving me rooted to the spot. She wasn't here. She hadn't been here. Then where the hell was she?

"Are you sure?" I asked, my voice low and urgent. "She hasn't been here at all? Not since—" I stopped myself, realizing how desperate I sounded.

The servant shook his head, his expression apologetic. "No, my lord. We haven't seen Lady Ashford."

Panic gripped me as I turned and walked back to my horse, my mind racing. If she wasn't here and she wasn't at Ashford Manor, then where could she be? She couldn't have just vanished into thin air. Someone had to know where she was.

I mounted my horse, my heart pounding as I rode away from the estate, the dread deepening with every passing second. The possibilities raced through my mind, each one worse than the last. Had she run away? Had something happened to her? The thought of her being out there, alone and vulnerable, filled me with a fear I couldn't suppress.

And then, the unthinkable crossed my mind—what if she had done something drastic? What if she had decided that life wasn't worth living anymore, that the lies and the pain were too much to bear? The idea struck me like a physical blow, nearly knocking the wind out of me. No, it couldn't be. She wouldn't do that... would she?

But I couldn't shake the thought, couldn't ignore the gnawing fear that something terrible had happened. I needed to find her, and I needed to find her now.

I rode hard, my thoughts a tangled mess of worry and regret. I had let my pride and anger blind me, had refused to see the pain she was in. And now, she was gone, and it was my fault.

I had to find her. I had to make sure she was safe, that she was all right. Because the truth was, no matter how much she had hurt me, no matter how deep the betrayal ran, I still cared about her. And the thought of losing her for good was something I couldn't bear.

The sun was setting as I arrived back at Ashford Manor, the light fading fast as I dismounted and stormed into the house. The servants looked up in surprise as I burst through the door, but I didn't stop to explain. I headed straight for my study, determined to figure out where she might be.

But as I reached the door, I stopped, my hand hovering over the doorknob. For the first time in two weeks, I allowed myself to feel the full weight of my emotions. The fear, the regret, the guilt—they all crashed down on me, overwhelming me with their intensity.

I had driven her away. I had let my anger and pride push her to the point of breaking, and now she was gone. And if something had happened to her—if she was hurt or worse—I would never forgive myself.

I took a deep breath, steeling myself for what lay ahead. I had to find her, no matter what it took. I had to make sure she was safe, that she knew she wasn't alone. Because despite everything, despite the lies and the pain, I still loved her. And I couldn't lose her now.

With renewed determination, I pushed open the door to my study and began to plan my next move. I wouldn't rest until I found her, until I knew she was safe. And when I did, I would do whatever it took to make things right.

Because the truth was, I couldn't bear the thought of a world without Anne in it. And I was willing to fight to keep her, even if it meant confronting the demons of our past.

38

The Confrontation

The anxiety that had been gnawing at me for days had reached a fever pitch. I couldn't sit still, couldn't focus on anything but the gnawing fear that something had happened to Anne. The thought of her out there, lost or hurt, was more than I could bear. I had to find her, and I was running out of places to look.

With a heart heavy with dread, I rode to Lightwood Manor, my mind racing with the possibilities. I hadn't wanted to involve Duke Bastian or Adelaide in this, but I was desperate. I needed answers, and I needed them now.

As soon as I arrived, I was met by a servant who looked at me with wide eyes, clearly taken aback by my sudden appearance. I didn't have time for formalities.

"Where is she?" I demanded, my voice sharp with desperation. "Where is Anne?"

The servant stammered, but before he could answer, I heard the heavy footsteps of someone approaching. I turned to see Duke Bastian himself striding toward me, his expression thunderous. I barely had time to react before his fist connected with my jaw, sending me stumbling back.

The force of the blow shocked me, and I tasted blood as I caught myself against the wall. Bastian's eyes were blazing with anger, his normally composed demeanor shattered by a fury that matched my own desperation.

"I warned you," Bastian growled, his voice low and dangerous. "I warned you not to mess with Anne. You hurt her, and in doing so, you nearly cost me my wife and child. You've gone too far, Colin."

I wiped the blood from my lip, my heart pounding not just from the physical blow but from the realization of how much damage I had done. "Bastian, I'm sorry," I said, my voice hoarse with emotion. "I know I've made mistakes, but I need to see her. I need to know she's all right."

Bastian's eyes narrowed, his anger barely contained. "She's not here, Colin," he said coldly. "And even if she were, I wouldn't let you near her."

"I don't believe you," I shot back, the desperation clawing at me. "She has to be here. Where else would she go? Let me see her—let me see Adelaide, and I'll leave."

Bastian's expression darkened further, and for a moment, I thought he might strike me again. "You're not seeing anyone," he snapped. "You've done enough damage. Anne isn't here, and Adelaide needs rest, not more of your drama."

But I couldn't give up. I couldn't just walk away, not when I was so sure that Anne was somewhere in this manor. I had to find her, had to make sure she was safe. Ignoring Bastian's warning, I pushed past him and ran into the manor, my heart racing with panic.

"Anne!" I shouted, my voice echoing through the grand halls. "Anne, where are you?"

I ran from room to room, my footsteps echoing in the silence. But no matter where I looked, Anne was nowhere to be found. My calls went unanswered, and with each empty room, my fear grew.

"Anne!" I called again, my voice cracking with desperation.

But then, as I reached the end of a long corridor, the door to one of the rooms opened, and Adelaide stepped out. Her face was pale, her expression a mixture of exhaustion and anger. She was still recovering from the difficult birth, and seeing her in this state only deepened my guilt.

"Anne isn't here, Colin," Adelaide said, her voice cold. "You need to leave."

Her words hit me like a punch to the gut, and for a moment, I just stood there, my mind reeling. "Adelaide, please," I pleaded, my voice trembling. "I need to know she's all right. Where is she?"

THE CONFRONTATION

Adelaide's eyes flashed with anger, and she shook her head. "You don't deserve to know where she is," she said, her voice sharp. "After everything you've done, you've lost the right to ask about her. Now, leave. You've caused enough harm."

Her words cut deep, and I realized there was no point in arguing. I had lost this battle. I couldn't push her any further, not when she was so clearly angry and protective of her sister. But even as I turned to leave, a part of me refused to give up.

I would come back. I would find Anne. Because I was certain—despite what Bastian and Adelaide said—that she was here, somewhere. And I wouldn't rest until I found her and made things right.

As I walked out of the manor, Bastian's words echoed in my mind, mingling with the fear that had been gnawing at me for days. I had hurt Anne, driven her to the point of disappearance, and in doing so, I had nearly lost everything. But I couldn't lose her now. Not when I was finally realizing how much she meant to me.

I had to find her. I had to make things right, no matter what it took.

39

The Desperate Search

The sun had barely risen when I found myself once again at the gates of Lightwood Manor, my heart heavy with the weight of the previous day's failures. The desperation gnawed at me, a constant, insistent ache that refused to let me rest. I needed to see Anne, needed to know she was safe, and I wouldn't stop until I did.

But as I approached the grand entrance, the manor seemed cold and unwelcoming, the windows dark, the air thick with an unspoken refusal. When I knocked, the door was opened by a stern-faced servant who informed me that neither Duke Bastian nor Adelaide would see me.

"They've made their wishes clear, my lord," the servant said, his tone respectful but firm. "You are not welcome here."

I clenched my fists at my sides, fighting the rising tide of frustration and fear. "I just need to speak with Anne," I said, my voice betraying the desperation I felt. "Please, I need to make things right."

But the servant merely shook his head. "Lady Ashford is not here, my lord. I'm sorry, but there's nothing more I can do for you."

I didn't believe him. I couldn't. Anne had to be here—where else would she go? Ignoring the servant's words, I tried to push past him, determined to search the manor myself if I had to, but he stepped in front of me, blocking my way.

"Please, my lord," the servant said, his voice gentle but unyielding. "You need to leave."

I stared at him, my breath coming in ragged gasps as the realization began to sink in. They weren't going to let me see her. They weren't going to let me make things right. I had failed again.

With a heavy heart, I turned away and left the manor, my mind a whirl of confusion and despair. But I couldn't give up. I wouldn't. So, the next day, I returned, and the day after that, each time hoping that they would change their minds, that they would let me see her, that they would let me explain. But each time, I was met with the same cold refusal.

I was becoming a ghost of myself, the desperation clawing at me, tearing me apart from the inside. I couldn't sleep, couldn't eat, couldn't think of anything but finding Anne. Every time I closed my eyes, I saw her face, pale and exhausted, filled with the pain I had caused her. I replayed our last conversation over and over in my mind, the memory of her confession haunting me, driving me to the brink of madness.

On the fifth day, as I stood at the gates of Lightwood Manor, I was approached by a young servant—a boy no older than fifteen—who looked at me with wide, nervous eyes.

"My lord," he said hesitantly, glancing around as if afraid he might be caught. "I have a message for you."

My heart leaped in my chest. "What is it? Is it from Anne?"

The boy shook his head, looking down at his feet. "No, my lord. But I overheard the other servants talking. Lady Ashford isn't here. She left the manor the day after Lady Lightwood gave birth."

The words hit me like a physical blow, knocking the wind out of me. "She left?" I whispered, the shock rendering me almost speechless. "Where did she go?"

The boy looked up at me, his expression one of deep sympathy. "No one knows, my lord. She left in the night, and she hasn't been seen since."

I staggered back, the world spinning around me as the full weight of what he was saying sank in. Anne was gone. She had left the manor, and no one knew where she was. I had lost her.

"Thank you," I murmured, my voice barely audible as I turned away, the boy's concerned gaze following me as I walked back to my horse. I felt hollow, as if everything that had once held me together had been stripped away, leaving only a shell of the man I had been.

I mounted my horse and rode away from Lightwood Manor, the reality of my situation settling over me like a suffocating fog. I didn't know where else to look, didn't know where Anne could have gone. Every possibility, every lead, had been exhausted, and I was left with nothing but the gnawing fear that I had lost her forever.

The ride back to Ashford Manor was long and filled with the oppressive weight of failure. I had failed to protect Anne, failed to keep her safe, and now she was gone, lost to me in the dark unknown. The thought of her out there, alone and vulnerable, filled me with a terror I couldn't shake.

When I arrived back at Ashford Manor, I was greeted by the familiar, oppressive silence that had settled over the house in Anne's absence. The servants moved quietly, their faces etched with concern, but I couldn't bring myself to speak to them. I couldn't bear the thought of answering their unspoken questions, of explaining that I had lost the woman I had vowed to protect.

I went straight to my study, the one place where I could be alone with my thoughts, where I could try to make sense of the chaos that had become my life. But as I sat there, staring blankly at the papers scattered across my desk, I realized there was no sense to be made. I had pushed Anne away, driven her to the point of disappearing, and now she was gone, with no trace left behind.

The days stretched into an endless blur, each one marked by the same hollow ache in my chest, the same gnawing fear that I had lost Anne forever. I searched everywhere I could think of, questioned anyone who might have seen her, but there was nothing. No clues, no leads—just an overwhelming emptiness that left me reeling.

The truth was, I didn't know how to go on without her. I didn't know how to live with the knowledge that I had driven her away, that my own anger and pride had cost me the one thing I had come to realize I couldn't live without.

And so, I waited. I waited and hoped that, somehow, she would find her way back to me. That, somehow, we could find a way to fix the mess we had made. But with each passing day, that hope grew fainter, and I began to fear that I might never see her again.

The realization was a bitter pill to swallow, but it was one I couldn't ignore. I had lost Anne, and I had no one to blame but myself.

40

A Glimmer of Hope

The days blurred together into an endless cycle of desperation and despair. Anne had been gone for months now, and with each passing day, the hope that I might find her grew dimmer. I searched relentlessly, scouring every corner of London, attending every social event I could, questioning anyone who might have seen her. But it was as if she had vanished into thin air, leaving no trace behind.

The strain of it all took a toll on me. I hardly slept, hardly ate, my mind consumed by the need to find her, to bring her back. My body began to betray me, growing weaker with each passing day. I became a shadow of myself, my skin pale, my frame gaunt. Even the simple act of eating turned into an ordeal. Every morning, I woke up with a wave of nausea, unable to keep anything down. I felt dizzy, lightheaded, but none of it mattered. I would endure anything, suffer anything, if it meant I could find Anne.

Harris, my loyal butler, was beside himself with worry. He watched me with concern, his brow furrowed as he tried to coax me into eating, into resting. But I brushed off his concerns, too focused on my search to care about my own well-being.

"My lord," Harris said one morning as I pushed away the breakfast he had brought, unable to stomach the sight of it. "You must take care of yourself. You won't be able to find Lady Ashford if you're too ill to stand."

"I'll be fine," I muttered, clutching the edge of the table as another wave of dizziness washed over me. "I just need to find her. That's all that matters."

But even as I spoke the words, I knew they were a lie. I wasn't fine, not by any stretch of the imagination. My body was failing me, weakened by the relentless stress and lack of proper care. But I couldn't stop, couldn't give up, not when Anne was still out there, alone and vulnerable.

As the weeks turned into months, my search grew more frantic, more desperate. I was running out of places to look, out of people to ask. Each dead end, each failed attempt to find her, only deepened the sense of hopelessness that gnawed at me.

Then, one morning, as I sat slumped in my study, too exhausted to even move, a letter arrived. Harris brought it to me with a somber expression, the sealed envelope a stark contrast to the chaos that had become my life.

"It's from Lady Lightwood, my lord," Harris said, handing me the letter.

I took it with trembling hands, my heart pounding in my chest. Adelaide. What could she possibly want? Had she found Anne? Did she have news of her whereabouts? The thought sent a rush of adrenaline through my veins, and I tore open the envelope, my eyes scanning the contents with fevered urgency.

The letter was brief, containing only a single word: *Whitby*.

My breath caught in my throat as the meaning of that single word sank in. Whitby. A small, coastal village far from London, nestled on the edge of the Yorkshire coast. A place so remote, so isolated, that it was no wonder I hadn't been able to find her.

Anne was in Whitby.

The realization hit me like a bolt of lightning, sending a jolt of energy through my tired, battered body. Whitby. Of course. It made perfect sense. Anne had fled to the countryside, far from the prying eyes of London society, to a place where no one would think to look for her.

Without a moment's hesitation, I jumped to my feet, the dizziness and nausea momentarily forgotten. I had to go to her. I had to see her, to make sure she was safe. The thought of finally finding her, after all these months of searching, filled me with a sense of urgency I hadn't felt in weeks.

"Harris," I called, my voice hoarse from disuse. "Prepare my horse. I'm leaving for Whitby immediately."

"My lord," Harris began, his tone laced with concern. "You're in no condition to travel. Please, at least rest for a few hours before you leave."

"There's no time," I snapped, brushing past him as I headed for the door. "I've wasted enough time already. I need to find Anne."

"But my lord—"

"I said there's no time, Harris!" I barked, my temper flaring. "Just do as I say!"

Harris hesitated for a moment, clearly torn between his duty to follow my orders and his concern for my well-being. But in the end, he bowed his head and nodded, retreating to make the necessary arrangements.

Within the hour, I was on horseback, riding hard and fast toward Whitby. The journey was long, the roads rough and unforgiving, but I didn't care. I pushed my horse to its limits, driven by a single, all-consuming purpose: to find Anne.

The wind whipped through my hair, the chill of the autumn air biting at my skin, but none of it mattered. My heart pounded with a mixture of fear and anticipation as I rode through the rolling hills and dense forests, my mind focused entirely on the thought of seeing her again.

As I neared Whitby, the landscape began to change, the rugged cliffs and crashing waves of the North Sea coming into view. The village itself was small, nestled in a valley between the cliffs, its stone cottages and narrow streets giving it a quaint, almost otherworldly charm.

But I didn't stop to admire the scenery. My eyes scanned the village as I rode into the center, searching for any sign of Anne. The locals looked at me with curious eyes as I passed, their expressions a mixture of surprise and suspicion.

I stopped in front of an inn, my heart pounding as I dismounted. The innkeeper, a middle-aged woman with a kind face, came out to greet me, her hands wiping flour from her apron.

"Good afternoon, sir," she said, her tone polite but guarded. "What can I do for you?"

"I'm looking for someone," I said, trying to keep the desperation out of my voice. "A woman. Lady Ashford. She might be staying here, or somewhere in the village."

The innkeeper's eyes widened slightly, and she hesitated before answering. "There was a woman who came through a while back," she said slowly. "But she didn't give her name, and she didn't stay long. She seemed... troubled."

My heart sank at her words, but I refused to give up hope. "Do you know where she went?" I asked, my voice trembling. "Did she say anything about where she was going?"

The innkeeper shook her head. "No, sir. She left early in the morning, before anyone had a chance to speak with her."

The crushing weight of despair settled over me, and for a moment, I felt as if I might collapse. But I couldn't give up. Not now. Not when I was so close.

"Thank you," I muttered, turning away from the inn and mounting my horse once more.

I rode through the village, asking everyone I met if they had seen Anne, if they knew where she might have gone. But no one had any answers. It was as if she had vanished into the mist, leaving nothing behind but a trail of uncertainty.

As the sun began to set, casting long shadows over the cliffs, I found myself at the edge of the village, staring out at the vast expanse of the North Sea. The waves crashed against the rocks below, the sound a constant roar in my ears, but all I could think about was Anne.

Where was she? Was she safe? Had I lost her for good?

The thought was too painful to bear, and I felt a tear slip down my cheek, the first of many that I had held back for too long. I had to find her. I had to make things right. But as the darkness closed in around me, I began to fear that I might be too late.

Whitby had been my last hope, and now it felt as if that hope was slipping away, like sand through my fingers.

But I couldn't give up. Not yet. Not until I had exhausted every possibility, every lead. I would search the cliffs, the moors, every hidden corner of this village if I had to. Because no matter how far she had run, no matter how lost she might be, I would find her.

And when I did, I would do everything in my power to bring her back home.

41

The Unexpected Reunion

The days blurred together as I scoured Whitby for any sign of Anne. Every corner of the village, every path along the cliffs, and every cottage nestled in the hills—I searched them all. My desperation grew with each passing hour, the fear gnawing at me like a relentless beast. I couldn't leave without finding her, but every lead seemed to evaporate, leaving me more lost than before.

By the time I reached the small, stone church at the edge of the village, my hope had all but faded. It was a humble place, with ivy creeping up the ancient walls and a simple wooden cross adorning the steeple. The kind of place where one might go to find solace, to escape the world for a time.

I tied my horse to a post and approached the heavy wooden doors, pushing them open with a sense of trepidation. Inside, the air was cool and still, filled with the faint scent of incense and candle wax. The church was empty, save for a nun who was arranging flowers at the altar.

She looked up as I entered, her face kind and weathered with age. "Good afternoon, my lord," she greeted me with a gentle smile. "What brings you to our little church?"

I hesitated, not wanting to burden her with my troubles, but I knew I had to ask. "I'm looking for someone," I said, my voice hoarse. "A woman who might have come here recently. She's... important to me."

The nun's expression softened with understanding. "We have many visitors, my lord," she replied. "But there is one young woman who comes here often. She doesn't speak much, but she's kind, always bringing bread or fruits for the children at the orphanage. She's with child, and I believe she is alone."

My heart leaped in my chest, and I struggled to keep my composure. "Is she here now?" I asked, my voice betraying the urgency I felt.

The nun shook her head. "No, my lord. She usually comes in the afternoon, to play with the children and tend to the garden. If you wish, you may wait here for her. I'm sure she will arrive soon."

The words "with child" echoed in my mind, leaving me stunned. Anne was pregnant. I hadn't even considered the possibility. The thought filled me with a confusing mix of emotions—shock, fear, and an overwhelming sense of heartbreak.

Pregnant. Was it possible? Had she left London to escape the scandal, to protect herself and the baby she carried? My mind raced with the implications, but I pushed the thoughts aside. I had to see her, had to confirm it for myself.

I nodded, unable to speak as the gravity of the situation settled over me. The nun led me to a pew near the back of the church, where I sat, my hands clasped tightly in my lap as I waited. The minutes ticked by slowly, each one feeling like an eternity. My heart pounded in my chest, the anticipation nearly unbearable.

And then, just as the afternoon light began to filter through the stained-glass windows, the door creaked open. I turned, my breath catching in my throat as I saw her.

Anne.

She stepped inside, her figure framed by the soft light of the setting sun. She was wearing a simple dress, her hair pulled back in a loose braid. My breath caught in my throat at the sight of her, the woman I had been searching for endlessly. Anne didn't see me at first. She walked down the aisle, her steps slow and deliberate as she approached the altar. She set down a basket filled with bread and apples, her movements careful as she knelt to pray.

I couldn't take my eyes off her. The woman I had been searching for, the woman I had driven away with my anger and pride, was here, right in front of me. I struggled to breathe, to make sense of the emotions swirling within me. The pain of losing her, the fear for her safety, the anger at her deception—all of it was eclipsed by the overwhelming love I still felt for her. But my heart clenched when I saw the unmistakable swell of her belly beneath her dress.

Anne was pregnant.

I felt as though the ground had been pulled out from beneath me. It was true. She was pregnant. My heart ached with a mixture of sorrow and disbelief. How could this be?

For a moment, the world seemed to tilt around me. I had spent months imagining this reunion, but nothing could have prepared me for this. I struggled to reconcile the woman in front of me with the Anne I had known, the one who had told me she wasn't pregnant just before she disappeared.

My mind raced, questions and doubts clawing at me with relentless force. How far along was she? Her belly looked like she was a few months pregnant—two, maybe three. But that didn't make sense. The timing didn't add up. If she had gotten pregnant after being in Whitby, her belly wouldn't have been that big. Or she had been pregnant when she left?

And then the darker thoughts began to creep in, the ones I tried desperately to push away. What if this wasn't my child? What if, after she left, Anne had found someone else? What if this was the result of a relationship she had formed after leaving me behind? Could Anne have gotten pregnant with another man as soon as she arrived in Whitby?

The doubt gnawed at me, poisoning the relief I had felt at finding her. I needed answers, but the fear of what those answers might be made my heart pound in my chest. I couldn't ignore it any longer.

Without thinking, I stood and walked down the aisle toward her. My footsteps echoed in the quiet church, and finally, she turned and saw me.

Her eyes widened in shock, her hand flying to her mouth as if to stifle a gasp. "Colin," she whispered, her voice trembling with disbelief.

For a moment, neither of us moved. We simply stared at each other, the weight of the months of separation pressing down on us. I saw the fear in her eyes, the uncertainty, and it broke my heart.

"Anne," I said, my voice thick with emotion as I took a step closer. "I've been looking for you everywhere."

She stood slowly, her hands trembling as she held them over her swollen belly. "What are you doing here?" she asked, her voice wavering.

"I came to find you," I said, struggling to keep my composure. "I came to apologize, to make things right."

Tears welled up in her eyes, and she shook her head, as if unable to believe what she was hearing. "How did you find me?"

"Adelaide," I replied, the single word heavy with meaning. "She sent me a letter. I didn't know where else to look."

Anne's gaze dropped to the floor, and I could see the turmoil in her expression. She was trying to be strong, to keep her emotions in check, but the sight of her standing there, pregnant and alone, was almost more than I could bear.

I took another step closer, reaching out to her. "Anne, please," I said, my voice breaking. "I know I've hurt you, and I'm so sorry. But I can't lose you."

She looked up at me then, her eyes filled with a mixture of pain and longing. "You were so angry, Colin," she whispered. "You pushed me away. I didn't know what else to do."

The memory of my anger, of the way I had treated her, made me flinch. "I was wrong," I admitted, my voice raw with regret. "I was so blinded by my own pride and hurt that I couldn't see what was right in front of me. But... is it mine?"

My eyes fell on Anne's stomach. Anne's gaze now dropped to her pregnant belly and held it with both hands. As she looked at me again, her eyes widened in shock, and I saw the hurt flash across her face before it hardened into something colder. "What did you just say?" she asked, her voice trembling with anger.

I hesitated, but the words were already out. "You said you weren't pregnant the night before you left," I continued, forcing myself to meet her gaze. "And now... seeing you like this, I have to know, Anne. Is this my child? Or did you... did you find someone else?"

Her expression darkened, and I immediately regretted the question. The look of betrayal in her eyes was like a dagger to my heart, and I wished I could take the words back. But it was too late.

"How dare you," she whispered, her voice shaking with a mix of fury and pain. "How dare you come here, after all these months, and accuse me of something like that?"

"Anne, please," I tried to reach out to her, but she pulled away, her face contorted with anger and grief. "I just need to understand—"

"Understand what?" she snapped, her eyes flashing with rage. "That you left me with no choice? That I had to run because I couldn't bear the way you looked at me, the way you pushed me away? And now, after all this time, you think I've been with someone else? That this baby isn't yours?"

Tears welled up in her eyes, and she turned away from me, her shoulders shaking with barely contained sobs. I felt the sting of my own guilt cutting through me like a knife, realizing the depth of the hurt I had caused her.

"I'm sorry," I said, my voice breaking. "I just... I've been so lost without you, Anne. I didn't know what to think."

She shook her head, tears spilling down her cheeks as she brushed past me, heading for the door. "Just leave, Colin," she whispered, her voice thick with emotion. "You've already made it clear how little you think of me. There's nothing more to say."

Panic surged within me as I watched her walk away, her figure trembling with each step. I couldn't let her go, not like this. I had come too far, and despite my doubts, despite everything, I couldn't bear the thought of losing her again.

I hurried after her, reaching out to grab her arm just as she reached the door. "Anne, wait," I pleaded, my voice desperate. "Please don't go."

She stopped, her back to me, and for a moment, I thought she might keep walking. But then she turned, and I saw the tears streaming down her face, the pain etched into every line.

"Why should I stay?" she asked, her voice trembling. "You don't believe me. You don't believe in us."

"I'm sorry," I repeated, my words filled with regret. "I know I've hurt you, and I know I've made terrible mistakes. But I'm here now, and I want to make things right. I want to be there for you, for our child."

She stared at me, her eyes searching mine for any sign of sincerity. "And what if it isn't yours?" she asked, her voice barely above a whisper. "Would you still stay? Would you still love me?"

The question hit me like a punch to the gut, and I realized the full extent of what she had been carrying, the fear and uncertainty that had driven her away. I couldn't let her carry that burden alone anymore.

"Yes," I said, my voice firm with conviction. "I would stay, Anne. I would stay because I love you, and I can't lose you again. No matter what."

Her breath hitched, and she looked away, her hand resting on her swollen belly. "You don't have to," she whispered, her voice breaking. "You don't have to acknowledge this baby. I can raise it alone. You don't have to pretend, Colin."

The pain in her voice cut through me, and I felt a deep, wrenching guilt for the doubts I had allowed to fester. I moved closer, gently placing my hands on her shoulders, turning her to face me. "I'm not pretending, Anne," I said softly, my heart aching with the need to make her understand. "I want to be here for you. I want to be here for our child. Please, let me prove that to you."

Her resolve crumbled in that moment, and she collapsed against me, sobbing into my chest. I held her tightly, my heart breaking with each tear she shed. I had hurt her so deeply, had driven her to the edge with my mistrust, but I was determined to make it right.

"I'm sorry," I whispered, pressing a kiss to her hair. "I'm so sorry, Anne. I should never have doubted you."

She clung to me, her sobs gradually subsiding as we stood there, wrapped in each other's arms. The church was quiet, the only sound the faint rustle of the wind outside. I knew that our journey to healing would be long, that the road ahead would be difficult, but in that moment, I made a silent vow to myself: I would not let go. I would fight for her, for us, and for the family we were about to become.

"I love you, Anne," I whispered, my voice thick with emotion. "And I'm not going anywhere. I'm here, for you and our child, no matter what."

She looked up at me, her eyes filled with a mixture of hope and fear. "Promise?" she asked, her voice trembling.

"Promise," I replied, my heart swelling with the sincerity of my words.

And for the first time in months, I felt a sense of peace settle over me. I had found her, and now, I would do whatever it took to keep her. Together, we would face whatever challenges lay ahead.

42

A Simple Sanctuary

The walk to Anne's home was quiet, filled with the unspoken tension of everything that had just transpired. The sun was setting, casting a warm, golden light over the village of Whitby, but I barely noticed. My thoughts were consumed by the woman walking beside me, her steps slower and more careful now that she was carrying our child. I couldn't tear my eyes away from her, from the way her dress clung to the gentle curve of her belly, from the way her hand rested protectively over it.

When we reached the small cottage that had been her refuge for these long months, my heart clenched painfully. It was a humble place, nestled among the other modest homes on the outskirts of the village. The walls were made of weathered stone, the roof thatched with straw. It was a far cry from the grandeur of the estate where she had grown up, or even from Ashford Manor, and the thought of her living here alone, pregnant and without the comforts she was used to, nearly broke me.

"This is where you've been staying?" I asked, unable to keep the sadness from my voice.

Anne nodded, her expression a mix of pride and resignation. "It's not much," she admitted, "but it's been enough. It's quiet, and no one here knows who I am."

The simplicity of her words struck me, and I felt a wave of guilt wash over me. She had been forced to leave behind everything she knew, everything she deserved, and all because of me. I had driven her to this, driven her to a place where she felt she had no choice but to hide.

I followed her inside, my heart heavy as I took in the sparse furnishings. The cottage was clean and well-kept, but there was no mistaking the fact that it was a place of necessity, not comfort. A small bed sat against one wall, a wooden table with two chairs beside it. A fireplace crackled in the corner, providing warmth in the cool evening air.

Anne moved with a practiced ease, lighting a candle and setting it on the table. "Let me prepare something for you," she said, her voice gentle as she moved toward the small kitchen area. "You must be hungry after such a long journey."

But the sight of her bustling around the kitchen, her hands busy with pots and pans, filled me with a deep sense of sorrow. This was my wife, the woman I had vowed to protect and cherish, and here she was, preparing a meal in this tiny, humble home, carrying my child, and doing it all alone.

"Anne, stop," I said, my voice thick with emotion as I crossed the room to her side. I gently took the pot from her hands and set it down on the counter. "You don't need to do this. I'm not hungry."

She looked up at me, her eyes searching mine for a moment before she nodded, her shoulders sagging with exhaustion. I could see the toll that the past months had taken on her, the way her body seemed to carry the weight of everything she had been through.

"Come here," I murmured, guiding her to the small bed in the corner of the room. I sat down and pulled her gently onto my lap, wrapping my arms around her as she leaned into me. Her head rested against my chest, and I felt the warmth of her body, the steady rhythm of her breathing as she finally allowed herself to relax.

We sat there in silence for a while, the only sound the crackling of the fire and the distant murmur of the sea outside. My hand found its way to her swollen belly, resting there as I felt the life growing inside her. The realization that I had almost missed this, that I had almost lost her and our child, hit me with full force, and I tightened my hold on her, as if afraid she might slip away again.

"It's been so hard without you," I whispered, my voice breaking with the weight of my confession. "I didn't realize how much I needed you until you were gone."

Anne was silent for a moment, her fingers tracing idle patterns on my chest. "I found out I was pregnant the day Adelaide went into labor," she said quietly, her voice tinged with a sadness that cut through me. "I was so focused on helping her, on making sure she was okay, that I didn't even notice how sick I was getting. And then, when I finally realized..."

She trailed off, and I could feel the tension in her body as she relived those moments. "I vomited violently and fainted. That's when I knew."

I closed my eyes, the image of her alone and afraid filling my mind. "Why didn't you come home?" I asked, my voice barely above a whisper. "Why didn't you tell me?"

She sighed, and I could feel her body trembling slightly in my arms. "How could I?" she replied, her voice tinged with bitterness. "I told you I wasn't pregnant, Colin. You didn't believe me then, and I knew you wouldn't believe me if I suddenly showed up and said I was. Especially after everything that happened with Earl Eric."

The mention of Earl Eric's name sent a surge of anger through me, but I forced it down, focusing instead on the woman in my arms. "I would have believed you," I said, my voice thick with regret. "I should have believed you. I'm so sorry, Anne."

She shook her head, her hand resting over mine on her belly. "You were hurt. I understand that. But I couldn't stay in London, not with the threats from Earl Eric, not with the way you looked at me. It was too much. Here in Whitby, I could be safe, even if it meant being alone."

The thought of her struggling through morning sickness, her belly growing each day without me by her side, made my heart ache with a pain I couldn't describe. "Was it difficult?" I asked, my voice barely more than a whisper.

She nodded, her voice trembling as she replied. "It was," she admitted. "But it was better than being in London, where I was constantly looking over my shoulder, constantly afraid. And I couldn't bear to see the coldness in your eyes, Colin. I couldn't bear it."

Tears welled up in my eyes as I realized just how much I had hurt her, how deeply my actions had driven her away. "I'm sorry," I whispered again, the words feeling so inadequate for the depth of my regret. "I'm so sorry, Anne."

She turned in my arms, her eyes meeting mine, filled with tears and something that looked like hope. "It's all right now," she whispered, her voice soft and forgiving. "You're here now. That's all that matters."

But it wasn't all right. I couldn't let her forgive me so easily, not after everything I had done, everything I had put her through. I leaned down, pressing my lips to her belly, feeling the warmth of her skin beneath my mouth. "I'm sorry," I murmured, my tears falling freely now. "I'm so sorry for everything, for not being there when you needed me. I'm sorry to you, little one, for not being the father I should have been."

The sob that escaped her lips broke my heart, and I wrapped my arms around her, holding her close as we both cried, the weight of the past few months finally crashing down on us. I had almost lost her, had almost lost everything, but now, in this small, humble cottage, I realized that I had been given a second chance.

"I love you, Anne," I whispered, my voice thick with emotion. "I love you so much, and I'll never let you go again. I promise."

She looked up at me, her eyes filled with a mixture of relief and love, and in that moment, I knew that we could get through this. We could heal, together, and build the life we had both dreamed of.

The road ahead wouldn't be easy, but as I held her in my arms, I felt a sense of peace settle over me. We had found our way back to each other, and that was all that mattered.

As the fire crackled in the hearth and the night deepened outside, I held Anne close, my hand resting on her belly, feeling the life we had created together. And for the first time in what felt like an eternity, I knew that everything would be all right.

43

Healing and Forgiveness

The tension that had weighed on us both for so long seemed to lift, replaced by a sense of calm that I hadn't felt in months. As I held Anne close, the conversation between us began to flow more easily, the heaviness of our earlier confessions giving way to something lighter, more hopeful.

Anne rested her head against my chest, her hand gently tracing the lines of my shirt as I continued to rub her belly in slow, soothing circles. There was something almost surreal about the moment—after everything we'd been through, sitting here together, finally beginning to heal.

"You know," I said, breaking the comfortable silence that had settled between us, "I think I finally understand why I've been feeling so sick lately."

Anne looked up at me, a hint of curiosity in her eyes. "What do you mean?"

I chuckled softly, though the sound was tinged with a touch of self-deprecation. "The nausea, the vomiting... I thought I was just coming down with something, or maybe it was the stress of everything that's been happening. But now, I think I might have been experiencing morning sickness along with you."

She laughed, a soft, melodic sound that warmed my heart. "Morning sickness?" she repeated, clearly amused by the idea. "But you're not the one who's pregnant, Colin."

"No," I agreed, smiling as I continued to rub her belly. "But maybe our baby is trying to give her stupid father a sign. Maybe she's just been trying to tell me to stop being so stubborn and come find you."

Anne's laughter faded into a gentle smile, her eyes softening as she looked up at me. "You're not stupid, Colin," she said quietly. "You were just in shock, that's all. I can't blame you for how you reacted. I'm the one who's been lying all this time, tricking you into marrying me."

She looked down, her expression clouded with guilt. "I had no reason to defend myself," she continued, her voice barely above a whisper. "I lied to you, deceived you, and then I ran away when things got too difficult. I'm so sorry, Colin. I never wanted to hurt you."

The pain in her voice tugged at my heart, and I leaned down, tilting her chin up so that our eyes met. "Anne," I said softly, "I forgive you. For everything. I know you were scared, and I understand why you did what you did. But what's important now is that we're here, together. And that's all that matters to me."

I could see the relief in her eyes, the way her body seemed to relax in my arms as the weight of her guilt began to lift. I leaned down and kissed her, a gentle, reassuring kiss that held all the love and forgiveness I had to offer.

"Just promise me one thing," I said as I pulled back slightly, my forehead resting against hers. "No more lies. No more running away. If something happens, if you're scared or worried, talk to me. We can face anything together, but I can't do that if you're not here with me."

She nodded, her eyes glistening with tears. "I promise," she whispered, her voice thick with emotion. "I'll never lie to you again, and I'll never leave without saying goodbye. I can't imagine life without you, either, Colin."

A wave of relief washed over me at her words, and I kissed her again, this time deeper, more passionately. The months of separation, the pain and loneliness we had both endured, seemed to melt away as I held her close, our lips moving together in a slow, heated rhythm.

But as the kiss deepened, a familiar desire stirred within me—a longing that had been building for months. It had been too long since I'd held her like this, too long since I'd felt her body pressed against mine. The need for her, both physical and emotional, was almost overwhelming.

I pulled back slightly, my breathing heavy as I looked into her eyes. "Anne," I murmured, my voice low and filled with longing. "I know it's been a long time, but... I want you. I want to be with you, if it's all right. I know you're pregnant, and I don't want to do anything that might hurt you or the baby, but..."

She smiled softly, her hand coming up to cup my cheek. "It's all right, Colin," she said, her voice tender and reassuring. "It's perfectly safe. I want you too."

The permission in her voice, the warmth in her eyes, was all the encouragement I needed. I leaned in and kissed her again, my hands sliding up her sides as I felt the heat between us grow. The months of distance, of fear and doubt, were washed away in that moment, replaced by the simple, undeniable truth of our love.

As I guided her down onto the bed, my hands caressed her gently, reverently, as if she were the most precious thing in the world. And to me, she was. This woman, who had endured so much, who had carried our child alone, was everything to me. And I would spend the rest of my life proving that to her.

We started with a deep, passionate kiss. Our lips met eagerly, and our tongues danced together as we tasted each other once again. I could feel the heat building between us, and I knew it wouldn't be long before we were in bed together.

I undressed slowly, savoring the moment. When I was down to my trousers, I approached Anne and gently began to uncover her modest dress. As I revealed her pregnant belly, I couldn't help but feel a wave of love and protectiveness. I knew I didn't want to hurt our baby, so I carefully straddled Anne, making sure to support her belly with my own.

Our bellies came into contact, and we both let out a sigh of contentment. I leaned down and kissed her again, more slowly this time. I could feel her breasts pressing against my chest, and I longed to touch them. But for now, I was content to just feel her warmth and closeness.

Very slowly, I began to insert my cock into hers. It was a tight fit, but it felt amazing. We moved together in a slow, steady rhythm, savoring every moment. I could feel Anne's breath on my neck, and her soft moans of pleasure only served to heighten my own arousal.

As we made love, I whispered sweet nothings into Anne's ear. "I've missed you so much," I murmured. "I love you, Anne. You and our baby mean everything to me."

Anne responded with moans of her own, urging me to go deeper and faster. We continued like this for what felt like hours, lost in our own little world. Eventually, I could feel myself getting close to release. I groaned and buried my face in Anne's neck as I came, filling her with my warmth.

Afterwards, we switched positions. I lay down on the bed, and Anne climbed on top of me. Her swollen belly looked so tempting that I couldn't help but reach out and rub it. "Hey, there," she said softly, so as not to startle our unborn child.

I couldn't wait to meet him or her and become a father. But for now, I was content to enjoy this special time with my wife.

As I continued to rub her belly, Anne's hands began to wander. She started playing with my cock, which was already growing hard at the thought of being inside her. "You like that, don't you?" she whispered in my ear.

I moaned in response, unable to speak. Anne took this as a sign to continue, and she began to stroke my cock with more urgency. I knew I couldn't hold out much longer.

Finally, I couldn't take it anymore. I grabbed Anne's hips and pulled her down onto me, impaling her on my cock. She gasped with pleasure as I filled her up.

Anne's big belly moved up and down as she rode me, her breasts bouncing with each thrust. I reached up and squeezed her nipples, causing her to moan even louder.

We kept moving like this, our bodies slick with sweat, until there was only the sound of moaning in the room. I could feel myself getting close to the edge, and I knew Anne was too.

With one final thrust, I reached release, filling her up with my cum. Anne's body fell on top of mine, spent and satisfied. We lay there for a few moments, catching our breath, before getting up to clean ourselves off.

As we lay in bed, our bodies entwined, catching our breath, I couldn't help but feel grateful. Grateful for Anne, for our baby, and for the chance to be with them again. I knew that no matter what the future held, I would always cherish this moment.

44

The Homecoming

The journey from Whitby to London took several days by carriage, each mile bringing us closer to home, closer to a life I had almost lost. As the carriage rattled along the way, I couldn't help but glance at Anne every few moments, a constant, protective worry gnawing at me. She was pregnant, and while she assured me repeatedly that she was fine, I couldn't shake the concern that something might happen during the long trip.

"Colin," she said softly, her hand resting on mine as the countryside sped past the window. "I'm all right, really. The baby is fine. You don't need to worry so much."

I squeezed her hand, trying to smile but knowing that the anxiety was still written all over my face. "I know," I murmured. "But I can't help it. I don't want anything to happen to you—or our baby."

She smiled, her eyes filled with a warmth that eased some of my fears. "We're almost home," she said, leaning her head on my shoulder. "And when we get there, everything will be fine."

I nodded, wrapping my arm around her and pulling her close. The sense of relief that flooded through me as she rested against me was undeniable. After everything we'd been through, after all the fear and uncertainty, the thought of finally bringing her back to Ashford Manor felt like the first step toward reclaiming the life we were meant to have.

THE HOMECOMING

When we finally arrived at the manor, the familiar sight of the grand estate filled me with a deep sense of comfort. This was our home, and it felt right to be here, to bring Anne back to where she belonged. As soon as we stepped inside, I wasted no time in calling for the physician, insisting that he check on Anne and our baby.

The physician arrived quickly, his expression calm and reassuring as he examined Anne. I hovered nearby, trying to stay out of the way but unable to hide the nervous energy that had been building in me since we left Whitby. The minutes seemed to stretch into an eternity as the physician completed his examination, his face giving nothing away.

Finally, he turned to me, a small smile on his lips. "You can relax, Lord Ashford," he said, his tone warm. "Both Lady Ashford and the baby are in perfect health. There's nothing to worry about."

The relief that washed over me was almost overwhelming. I let out a breath I hadn't realized I was holding, feeling the tension drain from my body. "Thank you," I said, my voice thick with emotion. "Thank you so much."

Anne smiled up at me, her hand reaching out to take mine. "See?" she whispered, her eyes shining. "I told you we were fine."

I nodded, leaning down to press a kiss to her forehead. "I know," I murmured. "But I needed to hear it from him too."

Before I could say more, there was a commotion at the door, and I looked up to see Duke Bastian and Adelaide entering the room. Adelaide's face lit up with joy when she saw Anne, and she hurried over to her sister, pulling her into a gentle embrace.

"Anne, thank goodness you're home," Adelaide said, her voice filled with relief. "We've been so worried about you."

Anne returned the embrace, her smile soft and reassuring. "I'm home now," she said, glancing over at me. "And everything's going to be all right."

While the sisters talked, I found myself face to face with Duke Bastian. His expression was unreadable, but there was a seriousness in his eyes that I hadn't seen before. He motioned for me to step aside, and I followed him to a quieter corner of the room.

"Colin," Bastian began, his voice low but firm, "I'm glad Anne is back, and

I'm glad you're both safe. But you need to understand something—you can't hurt her again. She's been through enough."

The weight of his words settled heavily on my shoulders, and I nodded, my gaze steady. "I know," I replied, my voice resolute. "I won't. I've learned my lesson, Bastian. I won't let anything like this happen again."

Bastian studied me for a moment, as if gauging the sincerity of my promise. Then he nodded, his expression softening slightly. "Good," he said. "Because I've already had a word with Earl Eric. He won't be causing any more trouble."

I couldn't help the flicker of satisfaction that passed through me at the thought of Bastian teaching Earl Eric a lesson. "Thank you," I said, meaning it more than he could know. "I'll keep my promise."

Bastian clapped a hand on my shoulder, a rare gesture of camaraderie between us. "See that you do," he replied, his tone lighter now. "Anne deserves to be happy, and so do you."

Bastian's words made my resentment towards him for stealing Adelaide disappear. From his attitude and attention, I knew why Adelaide chose Bastian over me. Bastian was a much better man than I was, and he knew how to love his wife.

With that, we rejoined the others, the room filled with a warmth that had been absent for far too long. But the reunion wasn't over yet. Not long after, Anne's parents arrived, their faces a mixture of relief and contrition. The Earl and Countess of Windermere had clearly been worried about their daughter, and their relief at seeing her home safely was palpable.

"Anne," her mother said, her voice trembling slightly as she approached. "We've been so worried about you. We didn't know if you were safe..."

Anne smiled gently, reaching out to take her mother's hand. "I'm sorry for worrying you, Mother," she said softly. "But I needed time to figure things out."

The Earl stepped forward, his expression more serious. "Colin," he said, addressing me directly, "I must apologize for what happened. I know things got... complicated, and I take responsibility for any misunderstandings."

I shook my head, meeting his gaze with sincerity. "There's no need to apologize," I replied. "If anything, I should be the one apologizing. I promised to take care of Anne, and I didn't. But I'm going to make sure she's safe from now on. You have my word."

There was a moment of silence as the weight of our words settled between us. Then the Earl nodded, his expression softening. "I believe you, Colin," he said. "And I'm grateful for it."

After the formalities were over and our guests had left, the house finally settled into a peaceful quiet. It was just Anne and me again, alone in our room, the tension of the day slowly ebbing away. We sat on the bed together, our hands intertwined as we talked softly, sharing the small, intimate moments we had been denied for so long.

"I love you," I whispered, brushing a strand of hair from her face as I looked into her eyes. "And I'm so glad you're home."

"I love you too," she replied, her voice full of warmth. "More than you know."

I leaned in and kissed her, a slow, tender kiss that held all the promises we had made to each other. When we finally pulled back, I rested my forehead against hers, feeling a sense of contentment that I hadn't felt in months.

"I can't wait to meet our baby," I murmured, my hand moving to rest on her belly once more.

She smiled, placing her hand over mine. "Neither can I," she whispered. "It's going to be perfect, Colin. I just know it."

And as we sat there, wrapped in each other's arms, I knew that she was right. Whatever challenges lay ahead, we would face them together. Our future was bright, and I couldn't wait to start this new chapter of our lives, with Anne and our child by my side.

45

Double the Miracle, Double the Fear

The days after Anne returned home were filled with joy, hope, and a growing sense of anticipation. But there was something else too—a gnawing worry that neither of us spoke of aloud. Anne's belly was much larger than I had expected, even for a woman as far along as she was. Every time I saw her, the sight filled me with both excitement and a creeping fear that something wasn't quite right.

As the days passed and Anne's due date approached, my anxiety only grew. I found myself watching her closely, noticing every wince, every shift of discomfort. And when the contractions finally started, that fear turned into full-blown panic.

It was early in the morning when Anne first felt the twinges of labor. We had barely slept the night before, both of us too excited and nervous to find any rest. When she shook me awake, her face pale and drawn, my heart nearly stopped.

"It's time," she whispered, her voice trembling with a mixture of fear and excitement.

I jumped out of bed, rushing to help her up as the contractions began to build. The midwife had been staying with us for days in anticipation of this moment, and within minutes, she was by Anne's side, guiding her through the early stages of labor.

But as the hours dragged on, the tension in the room grew. Anne's contractions were strong, her body working hard to bring our child into the world, but something wasn't right. Her belly was still so large, even as she labored, and despite her efforts, the baby wasn't coming.

I hovered nearby, trying to stay calm, but the sight of Anne in so much pain was tearing me apart. I wanted to help, to do something, anything, to ease her suffering, but all I could do was hold her hand and murmur words of encouragement as she struggled to bring our child into the world.

The midwife, a seasoned woman who had seen countless births, began to look worried. "The baby should have crowned by now," she murmured to herself, glancing up at me with concern in her eyes. "Lady Ashford, we need to keep you moving. The baby needs to come down."

Anne's face was etched with pain, but she nodded, determined to do whatever it took. I wrapped my arm around her waist, supporting her as she got to her feet and began to walk back and forth across the room. Each step was agony for her, her contractions coming in waves that left her gasping for breath. But she kept moving, her determination shining through even in her weakened state.

"It's okay, love," I whispered, my voice trembling as I tried to keep my own fear at bay. "You're doing great. We're almost there."

But the hours dragged on, and still, there was no baby. Anne's strength was waning, and I could see the exhaustion in her eyes as she clutched her belly, her breaths coming in ragged gasps.

And then, suddenly, everything changed.

We were making another slow pass across the room when Anne froze, her hand flying to her stomach as her eyes widened in shock. "Colin," she gasped, her voice filled with a new kind of fear. "It's... it's moving down."

Panic shot through me as I watched her clutch her belly, the movement inside her unmistakable. Without thinking, I scooped her up into my arms and carried her back to the bed, my heart racing as I called for the midwife.

"Something's happening," I said, my voice shaking with fear. "She says the baby is moving down."

The midwife hurried to Anne's side, her hands moving quickly as she assessed the situation. "All right, Lady Ashford," she said, her voice calm but urgent. "It's time to push. You can do this."

Anne nodded weakly, her face contorted with pain as she braced herself for the final push. I held her hand, my own fear and exhaustion forgotten as I focused on her, on the life we were bringing into the world.

"Push, Anne," I urged, my voice filled with a desperation I couldn't hide. "You're so close."

She gritted her teeth and bore down, her entire body straining with the effort. And then, finally, I saw it—the crown of our baby's head, emerging slowly as Anne pushed with everything she had left.

Tears filled my eyes as I watched, my heart swelling with love and pride. "That's it, Anne," I whispered, my voice choked with emotion. "You're doing it."

With one final push, our baby came into the world, her cries echoing through the room as the midwife quickly wrapped her in a blanket and placed her on Anne's chest.

"A girl," the midwife announced, her voice filled with warmth and relief. "You have a beautiful baby girl."

I leaned down, pressing a kiss to Anne's forehead as she gazed down at our daughter, tears streaming down her face. "She's perfect," I whispered, my heart bursting with love for both of them.

But just as I was about to kiss Anne, I noticed something was wrong. Anne was still clutching her belly, her face twisted in pain even as she tried to smile down at our daughter.

"Anne?" I said, my voice filled with concern. "What's wrong?"

The midwife moved quickly, her hands pressing gently on Anne's abdomen. Her expression turned serious as she realized what was happening. "There's another baby," she said, her voice calm but firm. "Lady Ashford, you're carrying twins."

The shock of her words hit me like a lightning bolt, my mind struggling to process what she had just said. Twins. We were having twins.

Anne looked up at me, her eyes wide with a mix of surprise and exhaustion. "Twins?" she whispered, her voice barely audible.

I nodded, my heart pounding in my chest. "You can do this, Anne," I said, my voice trembling with both fear and excitement. "You're so strong, and our babies need you."

The next hour was a blur of tension and fear as Anne prepared to bring our second child into the world. She was exhausted, her body pushed to its limits, but she found the strength to push again, her determination shining through as she fought to deliver our second baby.

I stayed by her side, holding her hand and murmuring words of encouragement as she strained to bring our child into the world. And then, finally, after what felt like an eternity, our second baby was born.

Another girl.

The midwife quickly cleaned and wrapped the baby before placing her beside her sister on Anne's chest. Tears of relief and joy filled my eyes as I looked down at the two tiny, perfect beings we had brought into the world.

Anne was exhausted, her face pale and damp with sweat, but she was smiling, her eyes filled with love as she gazed down at our daughters. I leaned down and kissed her gently, my heart swelling with pride and love for this incredible woman who had just given me the greatest gift I could ever imagine.

"I'm so proud of you," I whispered, my voice thick with emotion. "You're amazing, Anne. We have two beautiful daughters."

She smiled weakly, her eyes closing as she finally allowed herself to rest. "I love you, Colin," she whispered, her voice barely audible. "I love our girls."

"I love you too," I replied, my heart overflowing with emotion as I kissed her again, then turned to look at our babies. "And I can't wait to watch them grow up."

As I sat there, holding Anne and our daughters close, I knew that everything we had been through—every fear, every challenge—had been worth it. Our family was complete, and I was more determined than ever to be the husband and father they deserved.

46

A New Beginning

The warmth of the late afternoon sun bathed the garden in a golden glow, casting long shadows across the lush green lawn of Ashford Manor. The scent of blooming roses filled the air, and a gentle breeze rustled the leaves of the nearby trees. It was a perfect day, the kind of day I had once only dreamed of.

Colin and I sat on the old wooden swing that hung from the large oak tree at the edge of the garden, the seat swaying gently back and forth as we watched our twin daughters nestled in our arms. The soft creak of the ropes, the whisper of the wind through the branches above, and the faint cooing of our babies created a symphony of contentment that filled my heart to overflowing.

As I looked down at the tiny faces of our daughters, their perfect features softened by the glow of the setting sun, I felt a wave of emotion so powerful it nearly brought tears to my eyes. They were beautiful—our little miracles—born from a journey filled with pain and uncertainty, yet here they were, perfect and whole, resting peacefully in our arms.

Colin sat beside me, his arm wrapped around my shoulders, holding me close as he gazed down at our daughters with a look of pure adoration. It was a look I had seen more and more in the weeks since their birth, a look that spoke of a love so deep and unwavering that it left me breathless.

"They're so perfect," I whispered, my voice barely audible as I reached out to gently brush a lock of dark hair from one of the baby's foreheads. "I can't believe they're ours."

Colin smiled, his eyes never leaving the tiny faces of our daughters. "Neither can I," he murmured, his voice thick with emotion. "I keep expecting to wake up and find out it was all a dream."

I leaned my head against his shoulder, feeling the warmth of his body seep into mine as we sat there together, the swing gently swaying beneath us. "If it is a dream," I whispered, "I never want to wake up."

For a long moment, we sat in silence, content to simply hold our daughters and bask in the happiness that had finally found its way into our lives. The worries and fears of the past seemed so distant now, like shadows that had been chased away by the light of our love and the arrival of our little family.

But as peaceful as the moment was, it didn't last long. One of the twins let out a tiny, whimpering cry, her face scrunching up in that way that only babies can manage when they're upset.

Colin's reaction was immediate. "Oh no, no tears," he said softly, his voice filled with tenderness as he carefully shifted the baby in his arms, rocking her gently. "What's wrong, sweetheart? Daddy's here."

I couldn't help but smile as I watched him soothe our daughter, his big hands cradling her so carefully, his voice a low, calming murmur. It was still strange to think of Colin as a father, but he had taken to the role so naturally, as if he had been born to it. There was no hesitation in his movements, no uncertainty—only a deep, instinctual love that guided him.

The crying quickly subsided, and our daughter settled back into his arms with a contented sigh, her tiny fist curling around one of his fingers. Colin looked over at me, his eyes shining with a mixture of relief and pride.

"Crisis averted," he said with a chuckle, his smile widening as he leaned over to press a kiss to my cheek. "I think we make a pretty good team, don't you?"

I laughed softly, feeling a warmth spread through me that had nothing to do with the sun. "I think so too," I agreed, my heart swelling with love for this man who had become my partner in every sense of the word.

As the sun dipped lower in the sky, painting the horizon with hues of orange and pink, I knew that this was the life I had always dreamed of. A life filled with love, laughter, and the joy of watching our children grow.

Colin shifted slightly on the swing, pulling me closer as we sat together, our daughters cradled between us. "You know," he said quietly, his voice filled with wonder, "I never imagined I could be this happy."

I looked up at him, my heart overflowing with love. "Neither did I," I whispered. "But I'm so glad we found our way here."

He smiled, his eyes meeting mine in a look that spoke volumes. "Me too," he murmured, leaning down to kiss me softly. "Me too."

As we kissed, I felt a sense of completeness that I had never known before. This was our life, our family, and it was more beautiful than anything I could have ever imagined.

When we finally pulled apart, I rested my head on his shoulder once more, the soft creak of the swing and the gentle coos of our babies lulling us into a peaceful silence. The world around us seemed to fade away, leaving only the warmth of the setting sun, the rustle of the leaves above, and the steady, reassuring beat of Colin's heart beneath my ear.

And as I sat there, surrounded by the love of my husband and the joy of our children, I knew that no matter what challenges the future might bring, we would face them together. Because in this moment, with the golden light of the setting sun bathing us in its glow, I had everything I had ever wanted, and so much more.